Starring Dorothy Kane

by JUDITH CASELEY

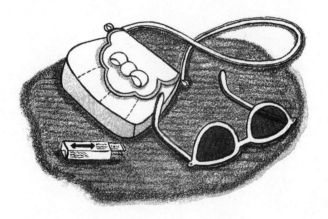

Greenwillow Books New York

Printed in the United States of America   First Edition   1 2 3 4 5 6 7 8 9 10

Library of Congress Cataloging-in-Publication Data
Caseley, Judith.
   Starring Dorothy Kane / by Judith Caseley.
       p.   cm.
   Summary: The adventures of Dorothy, the middle child, as she and her family move to a new house, she and her brother and sister go to a new school, visit their grandparents in Florida, and she makes a new friend.
   ISBN 0-688-10182-8
   [1. Family life—Fiction.
2. Moving, Household—Fiction.
3. Friendship—Fiction.]   I. Title.
PZ7.C26765St   1992
[Fic]—dc20
90-24172   CIP   AC

For SCH,
with love again

Contents

1

Dorothy, Not Like the One in *The Wizard of Oz*

WHEN DOROTHY'S PARENTS told Dorothy and Harry and Chloe that they were moving that summer, Dorothy felt a tiny bit excited. But just a tiny bit. Because she felt scared, too. The new house would never be as nice as their old apartment with the noisy elevator that she and Harry made believe was a spaceship. There would never be a better playhouse than her mother's walk-in closet. And Dorothy knew she would never find a best friend as nice as Stephanie.

"Stephanie always lets me be the mother or the princess," said Dorothy to her mother. "Whenever we play Mommy and Daddy, or Sleeping Beauty, or Snow White."

"I'm sure Chloe will play with you until you make new friends," said Dorothy's mother. "Then maybe you'll meet another little girl who will let you be the mother or the princess."

Dorothy shook her head. "Stephanie lets me wear the high heels, too. Chloe *never* lets me wear them. And she's *always* the mother." She put her hands on her hips and looked at Mrs. Kane.

Her mother sighed. "That's because Chloe is the oldest," she said. "You can always play with Harry."

"Harry is a big baby," Dorothy said, in a loud voice she knew her mother didn't like. "And he *always* gets his own way."

"We're *all* moving," said Mrs. Kane firmly.

2

"The subject is not open for discussion."

"There will never be a best friend like Stephanie," Dorothy said grouchily, but her mother was already walking out the door. "The middle kid never gets anything!" Dorothy shouted after her, but Mrs. Kane was washing dishes and she didn't hear a word.

When Dorothy's parents told her she could decorate her new room any way she wanted, she said, "No, thank you. I like my old room."

"With peeling paint?" said Dorothy's mother crossly. "And your brother Harry's indelible scribbles in marker all across the wall?"

"I like Harry's scribbles. They remind me of wallpaper," said Dorothy in an equally cross voice.

"But you can pick your own wallpaper," said Mr. Kane.

"I like paint," said Dorothy.

Mrs. Kane started counting to ten and left the room. Harry finished counting for her and said he would miss sharing a room with Dorothy.

"Harry sings to me," said Dorothy. "He has a really good voice."

"He can sing to you in the living room," said Mr. Kane, who hadn't lost his temper yet. "Or in the kitchen."

"Harry doesn't like the dark. I keep him from getting scared," said Dorothy. The truth was, Harry kept Dorothy from getting scared. When Harry woke up in the middle of the night and whispered, "There's a monster in the corner," Dorothy got up out of bed and pretended she was Supergirl, even though her heart was beating very fast. . . . She shooed the monster away, and when Harry looked at her and said, "You're the greatest!", she felt like the bravest sister in the world.

"Think of all the privacy you'll have," said Dorothy's father, "in your very own room."

Dorothy said, "I don't need privacy. I need company."

Mr. Kane shrugged his shoulders and said, "Well, you'll get used to it."

4

"No, I won't," muttered Dorothy when he left the room.

When the moving van pulled up to the new house, and Dorothy saw the front lawn with the pretty rosebush, she felt the smallest tingle of excitement. But she didn't tell her parents. Even when she saw the sunken living room again, which Harry reminded her looked very much like a swimming pool, Dorothy kept her mouth shut.

"We can have a big potted tree in the corner by the sunny window," said Mrs. Kane, running to the spot.

"Like the one in Uncle Peter's office," said Chloe.

"Nicer than that," said Mrs. Kane.

Dorothy was thinking that her little stuffed bird, Robin Redbreast, would look nice in the tree, but she didn't say so.

Then she discovered that the floors were so shiny and hard that you could slide on them in socks.

"We could make believe it's an ice-skating rink," Dorothy whispered to Harry. She couldn't keep herself from saying something.

"Watch out for splinters," said her mother, who had excellent hearing when it came to her children's whispers.

"I like our old carpeting better, anyway," said Dorothy, but it was getting harder and harder to hide her excitement.

Dorothy's bedroom was small, but it had frilly blue curtains in the window. They were much prettier than the mini blinds in the old bedroom she had shared with Harry. But Dorothy didn't say so.

"Is blue still your favorite color?" asked Mrs. Kane, tucking Dorothy into bed. "We can pick out a new bedspread together."

"If you want," said Dorothy. "But I love my Minnie Mouse quilt." She pulled the quilt up to her chin and said huffily, "And I won't throw it away."

"You don't have to throw anything away," said her mother.

Dorothy snuggled into her quilt. "Okay," she said in a small voice.

"Good-night, sweetheart," said Dorothy's mother, kissing her on the cheek.

"Mama?" said Dorothy as her mother turned to leave.

"What, dear?" said Mrs. Kane, smiling.

"Robin Redbreast would look good in that tree," whispered Dorothy.

"In which tree?" said Mrs. Kane, puzzled.

"The one in the living room."

"Oh." Dorothy's mother smiled again. "Do you like it here, just a little?" she said.

"Just a little," whispered Dorothy.

"I love you," said her mother, leaving the door open a crack.

Dorothy sat up in bed and looked around. It wasn't as scary as she thought it would be without Harry. It wasn't as lonely, either. She could play dress-up, and make believe she was an actress without Harry making fun of her. She could make up her own plays, and maybe Chloe would be the prince or the husband. Harry could watch. Dorothy reached out and touched the tip of her new blue curtains. Maybe a new quilt with cute little pigs on it would look nice. She decided that a small room was cozy. And privacy was nice. But she wouldn't tell her mother and father.

"Good-night, Harry," Dorothy called to her brother in the room next door.

"Good-night, Dorothy," Harry called back. "I have my new night-light on. It looks like a lightning bug."

"Good," called Dorothy. "I'm getting one to match my new curtains. Maybe it will be a pig."

"Good-night, Dorothy," called Chloe from the room on the other side of her. "We'll explore the backyard in the morning, okay?"

"Okay!" called Dorothy. "Maybe we could bury a treasure or something!"

"Maybe you can all go to sleep!" called her mother from downstairs.

When they woke up in the morning, they explored the kitchen first. Harry liked the fancy new watercooler in the corner. He poured himself a cupful from the little spout.

"What's the matter with the stuff in the faucets?" he said, drinking the fancy water. "It tastes the same."

"The spring water is purer," said Mr. Kane, putting a plate of scrambled eggs in front of Dorothy. "You don't like them too cooked, right?"

"She likes them wet and yicky," said Harry as he waited for his eggs to cook some more.

"Oh, gross," said Chloe, who munched on dry cereal and didn't eat eggs at all.

Dorothy shook some catsup on her eggs, and tasted a forkful. "Delicious!" she said, smacking her lips. Dorothy was glad that breakfast was just like it used to be in their old apartment. Except in the new house she could see how sunny it was outside by looking through the glass sliding doors into the backyard.

And after breakfast, they could step outside the sliding doors to play. They didn't even have to take an elevator. The yard was fenced in on all sides, which Chloe liked because she said they could play secret games without anyone watching. Dorothy liked their own private clothesline because she could hang a blanket over it and make a curtain for her plays. Harry wished he could see if their neighbors had any swings or slides or monkey bars, because that would mean they had children to play with. But it was impossible to see with a huge honeysuckle bush on one side, a tall wooden fence on the other, and a concrete wall at the back.

The side with the wooden fence had a dog. A loud, barking dog, scratching away at the ground as if he wanted to burrow his way right next door to the Kane yard.

"He sounds big," whispered Chloe, who didn't much like dogs.

"He sounds mean," whispered Dorothy, who only liked small dogs.

"He sounds friendly," said Harry, who liked any kind of dog that didn't bite. "He probably just wants to meet us."

Dorothy's mother came outside with her coffee cup. "Isn't this the life?" she said, leaning her head back and closing her eyes. She took a deep breath. "Fresh air." She opened her eyes again as the barking started up. "Whose noisy dog is that?" she said.

Dorothy laughed. "We say he's big and mean, and Harry says he's friendly."

"As long as he stays out of our garden," said Mrs. Kane, turning to go into the house.

"What garden?" said Dorothy, surveying the overgrown lawn.

"The one your father is going to plant," her mother said, laughing.

It was Dorothy's idea to be gardeners. She sent Harry inside to ask Mr. Kane if it was okay, and he came back out with three shovels and a watering can. "Dad says we can do whatever we want at the back of the garden. It's all weeds."

They took their shovels and set to work, pulling and digging and turning over the earth the way Harry had seen someone do on "Mister Rogers."

"That three-leaf clover should go over there," Harry said importantly.

"Just because you saw a program on gardening

doesn't make you the boss," said Chloe. Being the oldest, Chloe liked to give her own orders. "Besides, that doesn't look like clover to me. The leaves are too big."

Dorothy took her shovel and dug into the ground under the three-leafed plant. "It's kind of shiny and pretty, anyway," she said. "I'll plant it over there." Dorothy looked over at her sister to see if she minded, but Chloe didn't say a word, so she planted three of them in a row by the honeysuckle bushes.

Dorothy stepped back to admire her work.

"Mister Rogers would like it," said Harry.

Dorothy laughed. She was beginning to like living in a new house with a new backyard more and more. Maybe she would make a play about an enchanted castle with a beautiful garden, and she would be the princess. Maybe she would find a friend like Stephanie who would let her be the princess and wear the high heels. Her new friend would be the prince, and they would make crowns out of those pretty three-leafed plants.

Dorothy watered her garden until Harry said

it was lunchtime. Chloe ran inside and made peanut butter and jelly sandwiches while her mother made a pitcher of lemonade. Dorothy took out paper cups and a plate of cookies, and Harry found an old bedspread. They put it under the only tree with shade and had their first picnic in their new backyard.

Halfway through her sandwich, Dorothy heard shouting. "Get your butt in here, Benny Spignolli!" screamed a woman with a very loud voice.

"No way!" yelled a boy who sounded older and meaner than Harry.

"I hear a kid," whispered Harry.

"Mom's going to love it," said Chloe. "A noisy dog on one side—"

"And a noisy family on the other!" finished Dorothy with a smile.

"He's a few doors away," said Harry. "Maybe he likes playing Batman, like me." He took a chocolate chip cookie, dipped it in his lemonade, and ate it.

"Oh, gross," said Chloe, nibbling on her own

cookie and taking a sip of her ice-cold lemonade. She leaned back her head and closed her eyes, as she had watched her mother do. "This is the life," said Chloe.

Dorothy agreed.

But the next morning when Dorothy walked into the kitchen for breakfast, Mrs. Kane screamed and pointed a finger at Dorothy's face. Dorothy wasn't too surprised, because when she woke up, her face felt funny and itchy. It didn't help that Harry wrinkled up his nose in disgust and Chloe said she was going to barf up her breakfast.

"Poison ivy," said Mr. Kane, hitting himself on the side of his head. He opened the sliding doors and walked to the back of the yard in his slippers and bathrobe. Mrs. Kane and Chloe and Harry and Dorothy followed behind him. The whole family stood and looked at Dorothy's little garden of three-leafed plants.

"Poison ivy?" whispered Dorothy as she scratched her cheek.

"Poison ivy," said Mr. Kane, shaking his head. "I'm sorry, Dorothy. I should have checked what was back here."

"What's done is done," said Mrs. Kane.

"Go and see what was done to your face," said Harry.

Dorothy ran into the bathroom and looked in the mirror. It was worse than turning to the wrong channel on television and getting a scary movie. It was worse than any cartoon monster. It was Dorothy, with her face covered in red spots, her eyes swollen into tiny slits, and her neck a blotchy mess.

Mrs. Kane went into action. She called her new neighbor, Mrs. Peet, who lived next door to the noisy family, and got the name of a pediatrician. She called the doctor and got the name of a medicine. She settled Dorothy on the downstairs couch in the sunken living room, in front of the VCR.

"No sun," said Mrs. Kane, drawing the blinds. "And absolutely no scratching."

She pressed a button and *The Wizard of Oz* appeared on the television screen. Dorothy felt a little better. After all, Dorothy Gale was her favorite character in the whole wide world, and it was Dorothy Kane's belief that she had been named after her. It made a lot of sense. Dorothy Gale had long brown wavy hair, like Dorothy Kane, and she liked to wear blue. (Dorothy Kane had on her blue cotton nightgown that very day.) Dorothy Gale loved her little dog, Toto, and if Mr. Kane hadn't been allergic to dogs, Dorothy would have had her own dog named Toto, too. Dorothy Gale didn't have any brothers or sisters, but Dorothy Kane was very good at pretending she was an only child.

Of course, Dorothy's mother insisted that she was named after her great-aunt Dorothy on her father's side, but it didn't matter. Dorothy knew better. Great-Aunt Dorothy couldn't sing and dance the way Dorothy Gale could. And Dorothy Kane wanted to be an actress with all of her heart, not make the best chicken soup in the world, which her father said his Aunt Dorothy did.

But watching Dorothy Gale sing "Somewhere

16

Over the Rainbow," with her rosy-cheeked face that had no ugly rash on it, her big clear eyes that weren't slits, and her slim little dancing legs that weren't covered by itchy bumps, Dorothy Kane didn't feel much like singing and dancing. And when Dorothy fell asleep in the field of poppies, she certainly didn't catch any poison ivy.

As the movie came to a close, and Dorothy Gale said to Auntie Em, with tears in her eyes, "There's no place like home," Dorothy got tears in her eyes, too.

After all, there *was* no place like home . . . in her old apartment, with her old friend Stephanie, with no stupid garden, and no poison ivy.

First Day

DOROTHY STAYED INDOORS with poison ivy the entire week. The best day was the day it rained, because Chloe kept her company and no longer threatened to throw up whenever she looked at Dorothy's spotty face. They made believe they were mothers going on a shopping trip, with two carriages and two babies, and they even went out to lunch.

"Don't you dare throw another french fry on the floor," Dorothy said to her baby. "And you've got catsup on your chin." Dorothy dabbed at an imaginary blob of catsup.

"Nobody plays a mother like you do," said Chloe admiringly. "You even yell like a mother."

"When the sliding doors are open, I can hear Benny Spignolli's mother yelling at him. She gives me lots of ideas," said Dorothy. She turned to her baby and added, "And don't you dare spill your milk again!"

"Grandma is right," said Chloe. "You're a real actress."

"Of course I am," said Dorothy. "That's what I'm going to be when I grow up."

Chloe shook her head. "Not me. When I have to read a book report out loud in front of the class, I feel like I'm going to barf."

"Stage fright," said Dorothy, holding her baby doll against her and patting its back. "She burped!"

"That's exactly the way Aunt Milly does it!" said Chloe.

"Like I told you," said Dorothy, "I'm an actress."

On the morning of their first day at school, Harry was the only one who could eat breakfast. Chloe and Dorothy both complained of stomachaches, but their father instructed them to get into their new school clothes. He delivered them next door to Mrs. Peet's house and kissed them goodbye.

"Your mother would take you if she could," he said to Harry, who had tears in his eyes. "You know that Grandma is sick."

"So are we," said Dorothy, holding her stomach.

"That's nerves," said her father, hugging her once more. "You'll be fine."

But she wasn't. By mistake, she put her brother Harry in the second grade, the very same grade as herself, instead of kindergarten. And when the principal, Mr. Torres, stood in the doorway with Harry and asked Dorothy why she had done it, Dorothy's whole class laughed. Very loudly, it seemed to her. And the person who laughed the loudest was Benny Spignolli, her neighbor from two doors away, who was pudgy and spiky-haired, and looked as unpleasant as he sounded. Anyway, how was Dorothy to know that the number two in *2K* on the door meant the second grade? She figured that the *K* stood for kindergarten.

Once Harry found his real classroom and met his new teacher, he seemed to forget all about it. But Dorothy didn't forget. That very night, she dreamed that she put Harry into high school and her mother into kindergarten. She heard her mother yelling from behind a door with bars on it, "Get me out of here, I'm a mother, I don't belong in kindergarten!" Then a boy who looked like Benny Spignolli started laughing and pointing at her, and when Dorothy ran to open the door, it was locked. Dorothy woke up sweating, in a tangle of sheets.

The next day, when Mrs. Kane walked them all to school, Dorothy was sure that she heard

Benny Spignolli making rude noises behind her. She was sure that the tittering in the school yard was meant for her. What kind of dumb sister would put her little brother in the second grade?

"They're all laughing at me," Dorothy said from behind her hand to Chloe.

"They are not," said Chloe. "I'm the one who was supposed to watch over you and Harry, because I'm the oldest. It's my fault."

"No, it's not," said Dorothy, touching her cheek because she was sure some poison ivy spots had come back and that everyone would think she had pimples.

"It's my fault," said Harry. "I should have seen that all the kids were bigger than me."

Mrs. Kane started to laugh. "If I had been there, none of this would have happened," she said. "So it's my fault. I'm the boss and I say so."

But as Dorothy filed into her classroom with her eyes glued to the floor, she was convinced. They were still laughing at her.

Her teacher, Mrs. Greenaway, wrote something on the blackboard. "Family," she said.

22

"Who can tell me the different members of a family?"

Some of the children raised their hands. Dorothy thought it was an easy question. At home, she did a very good imitation of Grandma and Grandpa that made her parents laugh. But she stared at her desk and didn't move a muscle.

"Brother." Mrs. Greenaway wrote on the blackboard. "Sister. Grandmother. Grandfather. Mother. Father. Very good," she said, turning toward the class. Someone called out "aunt and uncle," and the teacher wrote them down.

Dorothy knew that they had left out "great-grandmother," because she had a Great-Grandma Fanny who was in a nursing home. But she didn't raise her hand, even when Mrs. Greenaway wrote "great-grandmother" on the blackboard and asked if anyone was lucky enough to have one.

"There are all different kinds of families," said the teacher. "I'd like each of you to stand up and tell us a little about yours."

A red-haired boy stood up. "I'm Joshua, and

we have a new baby who cries all the time, and my mother and father." Joshua sat down quickly, and stood up again. "And my mother's always tired," he added.

A girl with pigtails stood up. "My name is Andrea, and I live with my grandma and my mother. My father lives with his new wife, whose name is Gina, and my mother says she's too young for him." Andrea sat down.

A girl with a bright red bow in her hair stood up, right next to Dorothy. "My name is Jessica," she said, in such a tiny squeaky voice that Mrs. Greenaway asked her to speak up. "And I live with my mother—" Jessica stopped suddenly when someone called out, "And her mother sounds like a mouse, too!"

Mrs. Greenaway said sharply, "Stop the nonsense. Go on, please, Jessica."

Dorothy never found out if Jessica had a father or brothers and sisters, because some of the boys started squeaking like mice, and Jessica sat down so fast that the chair banged, and she looked as if she had no intention of getting up again. When Mrs. Greenaway gently asked her to continue, Jessica shook her head rapidly. That's when her red bow fell out of her hair, and one of the kids yelled, "She's falling apart!"

Dorothy felt sorry for Jessica, but she felt even worse when the teacher said, "Let's hear from Dorothy."

Dorothy stood up and gripped the edge of her desk. Her heart hammered as much as it did when Harry made believe he was a ferocious monster and jumped out at her from behind the bedroom door. "My name is Dorothy," she began. At least nobody started squeaking at her. Dorothy continued. "And I have a mother and a father and a sister and a . . ." Dorothy stopped. The word *brother* stuck in her throat.

"She has a brother who almost ended up in the second grade," said a voice from behind her that sounded like Benny Spignolli. Dorothy felt her face get very red. She sat down so quickly that she made a flapping sound on the seat.

"I will not tolerate rudeness in this classroom," said Mrs. Greenaway sternly. Dorothy held her breath when the teacher looked as if she was going to ask her to continue, but she called on Benny Spignolli instead. And nobody interrupted Benny.

Then and there, Dorothy vowed that she would never speak up in class again. Never never never. Which meant, of course, that she could never be an actress. Because if she couldn't speak up in class, then she couldn't speak up on the stage. And that's what actresses did.

The next morning, Dorothy told her mother that she didn't want to go to school.

"My stomach hurts," said Dorothy.

Mrs. Kane felt Dorothy's forehead. "You don't have any fever," she said. "Are you having trouble at school, honey?"

"No," said Dorothy. "I just hate it."

Mrs. Kane smiled. "I promise you it will get better. Haven't you met any nice children yet?"

"No," said Dorothy, shaking her head. "They're all nasty."

"They can't *all* be nasty," said Mrs. Kane, handing Dorothy her jacket.

Dorothy dragged herself to school and dragged herself into the classroom. When Mrs. Greenaway wrote a word on the blackboard, Dorothy felt her heart jump. Were they going to have to stand up and talk again? She raised her hand and said in a small voice, "Could I please go to the bathroom?"

Maybe Dorothy's voice sounded funny, because when she got out of her seat and walked to the doorway, Mrs. Greenaway met her there and said in a low voice so that the other children couldn't hear, "Are you feeling all right, dear?"

Dorothy felt her eyes well up with tears when Mrs. Greenaway called her dear, and she said, "My stomach hurts."

"Go ahead, honey," said her teacher. Dorothy went across the hall and into the room marked GIRLS. She sat in the stall for a long time. Maybe if she stayed long enough, she wouldn't have to stand up and speak in class.

Dorothy arrived at her classroom door just as the principal did. They walked inside together.

"What seems to be the trouble here?" said Mr. Torres. He sounded as though he was having as bad a day as Dorothy.

That's when Dorothy noticed Jessica, the little girl with the bright red bow. Jessica's head was stuck between the two wooden rungs of her chair. Mrs. Greenaway was hovering close by. The principal bent over Jessica. "What happened here?" he said.

"I dropped my eraser, and I took a shortcut to find it," said Jessica in a small voice. "I'm stuck."

"So I see," said Mr. Torres, laughing. "How come everything happens in this class?"

"Because we're an exciting class," said Mrs. Greenaway. "Right, Jessica?"

"Right," said Jessica. Dorothy thought she was trying to smile, but her cheek was pressing against the lower rung, so it was hard to tell.

"Right, Dorothy?" said Mrs. Greenaway.

"Right," said Dorothy, and it was her turn to smile.

"We don't want anyone to get bored. Right, class?" said Mrs. Greenaway.

"Right!" the class shouted in unison, and then everybody started to laugh, including Dorothy and Jessica.

Mr. Simpkins, the custodian, arrived with a toolbox in his hand. He took one look at Jessica and reached for his saw.

Jessica squealed when she saw it. "Please don't cut off my head," she said.

The class started laughing so loudly that Mr. Torres had to tell them twice to quiet down and move back, away from Mr. Simpkins. The custodian started sawing, and he promised not to cut off a hair of Jessica's head.

Dorothy was glad, because Jessica happened to have nice hair, short and brown and curly. Her red bow was vibrating slightly as Mr. Simpkins sawed back and forth.

"Don't cut off my bow, either," said Jessica, giggling this time.

"I'll hold your bow if you like," said Dorothy, looking around to see if anyone was about to make fun of her.

Mrs. Greenaway unfastened the bow. "That's nice of you, Dorothy," she said, handing the bow to her.

"Did you ever find your eraser?" said Joshua. Some of the children got down on their hands and knees and started looking for Jessica's eraser.

"Finished," said Mr. Simpkins, and he lifted first one side of the wooden rung and then the other. Jessica carefully raised her head, and everyone started clapping.

"I could have gotten her out of there," said Benny Spignolli.

Mr. Torres slapped the custodian on the back and said, "Well done, Mr. Simpkins. Do you think you can get Jessica a new chair?"

"You can share mine while you're waiting," said Dorothy, perching on the edge of her seat so that Jessica could sit next to her.

"No more excitement from this classroom," said Mr. Torres, smiling. "And welcome to the second grade!"

Dorothy turned and smiled at Jessica. "Here's your bow," she said.

Jessica smiled back. "You're new, aren't you?" she said.

"Yes," said Dorothy, making a face. "I'm the one who put her brother into the wrong grade."

Jessica laughed. "I'm the one who put her head into the wrong hole. Do you like bologna sandwiches?"

"Sure," said Dorothy.

"With mustard or mayonnaise?" said Jessica.

"With mayonnaise," said Dorothy, holding her breath.

"Me, too!" said Jessica.

"Do you like double-dipped Oreo cookies?" said Dorothy.

"My very favorite," said Jessica.

"We can share," said Dorothy, hoping her mother had remembered to put them in her lunch box.

"I can't wait," said Jessica. "I'm starving!"

That night, Dorothy watched *The Wizard of Oz* for the first time since she had gotten poison ivy. Dorothy and Chloe and Harry sat on the couch eating popcorn. Harry was the Scarecrow, because he was the smartest. Chloe was Glinda, the Good Witch of the North, because she liked wearing the crown. And Dorothy was Dorothy.

"You're just as good as she is," said Chloe, watching as Dorothy clicked her mother's high-heeled shoes together three times, saying, "There's no place like home."

"I am?" said Dorothy happily as she scrambled onto the couch for her final scene in bed. Harry remembered to put a cloth on Dorothy's head, like Auntie Em did.

Dorothy started her final speech. She didn't feel nervous at all, sitting up in bed as Harry and Chloe gathered around her. Maybe, just maybe, she wouldn't get the jitters speaking up in class again. After all, she had a new friend and a nice teacher, and school wasn't really *so* terrible.

Maybe she could be an actress after all.

"We're home, Toto," she said, clutching Robin Redbreast to her because she couldn't find a toy dog. "We're home, and I love everyone, and I'm never, ever going away again. Oh, Auntie Em," said Dorothy, hugging her sister Chloe. "There's no place like home."

And there wasn't.

3

Lost

IN THE MIDDLE of September, Mr. Kane called a family conference.

Dorothy and Harry and Chloe sat on the couch in their new living room. It was a Friday afternoon, and the sun was shining through the picture window onto Mrs. Kane's indoor tree. Dorothy considered it Robin Redbreast's new home, because most of the time he perched on the lowest branch.

"Is Grandma sick again?" asked Harry.

"No, thank goodness," said Mrs. Kane. "Your father wants to take a last vacation before the summer weather ends."

"During school?" said Chloe.

"Tonight!" said Mr. Kane cheerfully. "As soon as we can get ready. The weather report says it's going to be a beautiful weekend, and Uncle Bill is lending us his cabin."

"Hurray!" said Harry. "I'll wear my cowboy outfit!"

"What will we do there?" said Dorothy, who had been hoping she could play with her new friend Jessica.

"Hiking, a fire in the fireplace, bird-watching, roughing it. . . back to nature," said Mr. Kane. "Get out your school knapsacks, and we'll go pack."

Mr. Kane told them to take along a sweater and sweatpants, because the mountains could get cool in the evening. "We'll be back in time for school on Monday," he added, taking a floppy cloth hat out of the closet.

"Mom hates that hat," said Dorothy, laughing.

"I'm taking my hiking hat whether your mother likes it or not," said Mr. Kane, jamming it on his head with a smile. Dorothy thought he sounded just like Harry.

When her mother saw the floppy hat, she just raised one eyebrow and said, "I hope you won't wear it to bed." Sometimes Harry refused to take his cowboy hat off when it was bedtime, and he rested it across his eyes as if he was keeping the sunlight out.

They left the house without eating any supper and stopped two hours later at a fast-food restaurant.

"Are we there yet?" said Harry, a few minutes after they had gotten back into the car.

"No," said Mrs. Kane, unfolding a road map.

"Are we there yet?" said Dorothy, ten minutes

later. "It's getting so dark out I won't even be able to see the first cow."

"No," said Mr. Kane, settling his floppy cloth hiking hat on his head and switching on the radio.

"Are we there yet?" said Chloe, after listening to two songs. "I'm tired of looking for red station wagons."

"Whoever is thumping against the back of my seat, please stop!" said Mrs. Kane, who was beginning to get cranky, too. "We're almost there. Watch for the sign that says Beech Lake."

"Some cowboys can't read," said Harry.

"Look for the letter B," said Mrs. Kane.

Chloe spotted the sign first, but Dorothy said it was no fair, because Chloe could read better.

"You don't have to know how to read to go bird-watching," said Mrs. Kane, sounding a lot more cheerful.

"I'm going to find a giant bald eagle," said Harry, who had a picture of one on his bedroom wall.

"I'm going to find the first kingfisher," said Chloe, who had seen photographs of them at school.

"I'm going to find the first poison ivy," said Dorothy, laughing.

"And run the other way!" shouted Harry, waving his cowboy hat in the air.

The cabin didn't look like the log cabins Dorothy was used to seeing in the old cowboy movies. It had a fireplace, but there were no checked curtains, no horses tied to a post, no home-grown vegetables in the garden, no pictures of mountains on the walls, and no newly baked loaves of bread cooling on a wooden table. Harry found a peg to hang his cowboy hat on, and that made him happy.

Dorothy didn't think much of it. "It's ugly," she said.

"It's . . . plain," said Mrs. Kane, looking around at the scratched yellow plastic table, the four rickety cots, the rusty old stove, and the tiny refrigerator which made a loud humming noise.

Harry opened the refrigerator door. "It's empty!" he said. "We'll starve!"

"Where's the television?" said Chloe.

"There's no television," said Mr. Kane firmly. "That's why I told everybody to bring books."

"Where's the bedroom?" said Dorothy, counting the beds. "One of us doesn't have any place to sleep!"

"I'm the oldest," said Chloe, "so I need a bed."

"I'm the youngest, so I get one, too," shouted Harry.

"I have an idea," said Dorothy, but nobody paid any attention, because her mother was talking to her father, and Harry was lying spread-eagle across a cot, saying, "This one is mine," and Chloe was declaring that she would not, under any circumstances, sleep on the dirty disgusting floor.

"Won't somebody listen to me?" said Dorothy, and her mother put out a hand and said, "In a minute, Dorothy. We're trying to figure things out," and her father said that the cots were much too small for two of the children to share, and he wasn't sure if his back could take it if he slept on the floor. Dorothy opened her mouth and announced as loudly as she could, *"I have a great idea!"* and everybody turned to look at her.

Dorothy turned to Harry and said, "Cowboys don't sleep in beds, do they?"

Harry thought for a moment. "She's right," he said. "They sleep out on the plains. In a sleeping bag."

Mrs. Kane looked very relieved, and squeezed Dorothy's shoulder on the way out to the car, whispering, "Thank goodness I threw a sleeping bag in the back of the car."

Dorothy was glad, too, because the cabin looked like a great home for bugs and spiders, and sometimes the middle child had to do all sorts of nasty things, just because she wasn't the oldest and she wasn't the youngest. And Dorothy didn't like the idea of sleeping on the floor with spiders crawling all over the place, even if she *was* a great actress and could pretend she was a cowgirl even better than Harry.

Mrs. Kane returned with a box of groceries, and put the bread and eggs and milk in the tiny refrigerator.

"See, Harry? We won't starve," she said, smiling.

"And I discovered a little bathroom over there," said Dorothy, who was still thinking about bugs. "So we don't have to go in the woods."

Mr. Kane opened the door and laughed. "The size of a closet!" he said. Then he blew an imaginary trumpet, and Dorothy and Harry stood at attention like soldiers. "At ease, men and women," he said. "We're going to build a fire." He handed Dorothy some wood and told Harry to crumple up some newspaper. Mr. Kane tucked the paper in between the pieces of wood and lit a match to them.

The cabin looked much prettier now, with the flickering of the fire making shadows on the walls and on their faces as they gathered around the fireplace. Mrs. Kane brought them cups of milk and a plate of cookies, and they sat and listened to the crackle of burning wood and to Harry's noisy munching of oatmeal cookies and to Dorothy singing "Home on the Range."

Dorothy and Chloe brushed their teeth in the tiny bathroom and climbed into their creaky cots. Harry was already in his sleeping bag on the floor. Mrs. Kane made him brush his teeth there and handed him a bowl to spit into, even though Harry complained that real cowboys didn't brush their teeth.

Mrs. Kane tucked Dorothy into bed and gave her a kiss. "Thanks for helping us out back there," she whispered.

"I know all about Harry," explained Dorothy. "From when I shared a room with him."

"I'm sorry we didn't listen to you in the first place," said Dorothy's mother.

"I'm not the oldest," whispered Dorothy, "but I'm pretty smart." She pulled a scratchy woolen blanket up to her chin and murmured, "We should have brought my new pig blanket with us. It would have cheered up the place."

The next thing Dorothy heard was the screen door slamming. Sunlight was streaming through the window, and Dorothy was surprised that it was morning already and that she had slept the whole night through on the rickety cot.

Mr. Kane was busy unpacking a bag of groceries. He hummed as he ripped open a bag of bread and spread ten pieces across the scratched yellow table. Mrs. Kane slathered each piece with peanut butter.

"Can I help?" said Dorothy from her bed, thinking that she could pretend she was working in a factory. She got out of bed and stepped over a lump she knew must be Harry, who had burrowed down into his sleeping bag and was snoring like an old cowboy.

"You can do the jelly," said her mother, handing Dorothy a spoon.

Dorothy put a blob of jelly on each slice,

spread the purple mound carefully, and slapped a piece of bread on top of the jelly. Mr. Kane cut the sandwiches in half and wrapped them in waxed paper. Then Dorothy held her father's explorer knapsack open as he packed it full of sandwiches, juice boxes, raisin snacks, fruit, and two flashlights. He clipped a canteen of water to his belt.

"It's sunny outside!" said Dorothy. "What are the flashlights for?"

"We're going on a hike," said Mr. Kane. "The flashlights are in case of an emergency. It gets pitch-dark in the woods." He cracked some eggs into a bowl and called to Harry and Chloe. "Wake up, sleepyheads! Dorothy and I have been up for hours!" Then he winked at Dorothy and started scrambling the eggs.

Beech Lake Trail was not around the lake. It was up a very steep mountain. At first, it was fun following the blue trail markers posted on the trees, climbing up hills and around piles of rocks which Dorothy and Harry pretended were rattlesnake nests, through brambly bushes, and straight up the mountain once more. Mr. Kane led the way in his floppy hat. Then Chloe, Harry, and Dorothy followed, single file. Dorothy pretended she was a mountain guide, and she turned to her mother to point out a patch of tiny white flowers.

But her mother was gone.

"We've lost Mom," Dorothy called to her father. Then she chanted the hiking song Mr. Kane had taught them in the car. "Eee awk eee, answer me."

The bushes parted and her mother appeared. "I'm here," said Mrs. Kane, panting. She peered into the distance at the steep trail that lay ahead. "Are we there yet?" she said, nudging Dorothy.

"Stick with me," said Dorothy, taking her mother's hand. She pulled her mother uphill to the next tree. "I'll be your guide."

They rested for several seconds. Dorothy took her mother's hand again and pulled her up the steepest dirt incline yet. They had nearly reached the top when Mrs. Kane stumbled and fell. Dorothy held on to her hand tightly, but as her mother started sliding downhill, Dorothy lost her footing and landed on her backside, sliding after her mother as if she were on a sleigh ride.

"Help!" Dorothy's mother yelled up the hill, which started Dorothy laughing, and then her mother, so that every time they tried to pick themselves up, they fell down again. "Help!" shouted Dorothy, even though a mountain guide would never need any.

Dorothy managed to stand up before her mother did, and she waved to her father as she took hold of her mother's hand again. Mrs. Kane struggled to her feet, muttering, "I'm getting too old for this."

Reaching the top was only the first part of the hike, because they came to a crudely written wooden sign propped up against a tree: WARNING TO HIKERS: DIFFICULT TRAIL AHEAD. PROCEED WITH CAUTION. Mr. Kane looked at Mrs. Kane, who raised her eyebrows.

"Energy food!" said Dorothy's father, pulling five boxes of raisins out of his knapsack. "Eat! And then we proceed with caution."

"You're the leader," said Mrs. Kane, handing out the raisins. "And Dorothy, my mountain guide, will see me through."

The first part of the hike had rungs hammered into sheer rock that they had to climb up as if it were a ladder.

"Don't look down," warned Mrs. Kane between clenched teeth, but she was the only one left at the bottom, so Dorothy figured she must be talking to herself.

"I don't think I can do it," her mother called. Dorothy couldn't believe her own ears. Her mother could do almost anything, except for setting up the VCR or fixing the car. And if she couldn't do it, her mother's favorite saying was, "If at first you don't succeed, try, try again."

Dorothy's father seemed surprised, too. "Of course you can do it," he called down to her.

"Do you want me to come down and help

you?" said Dorothy, wondering how a mountain guide could help someone up a ladder.

"No," said her mother, gritting her teeth and starting to climb.

"This is supposed to be fun!" joked Mr. Kane, when she got to the top. Mrs. Kane rolled her eyes. She did it again when she saw the next part of the hike. It was the same sheer rock, but this time the rungs were anchored sideways, and hikers had to inch their way across a tiny ledge around the face of the rock by holding onto the rungs.

"I can do it, I can do it," said Mrs. Kane under her breath as she followed Dorothy. Dorothy's heart was beating quickly, but not the way it did when she had to speak up in class.

"You're doing great," said Dorothy. She felt very brave, shooing away the monsters for her mother like she did for Harry when he was afraid of the dark. Then she looked below her, and her heart jumped as she saw the tiny dots that were houses and the tiny specks that were sheep and the narrow winding ribbons that were roads. "Whatever you do, don't look down," she said to her mother.

"I won't," said Mrs. Kane, wiping away a drop of sweat that trembled on the tip of her nose.

"You're almost there," said Dorothy as she rounded the corner and saw her father and Harry and Chloe resting on a long flat boulder. She heard a scattering of stones as her mother's foot slipped. The stones disappeared quickly from view, and her mother held on to the metal rungs, white-knuckled.

Dorothy gently tapped her mother's hand. "One more climb, Dad says, and we're at the top."

"Will you live with me here instead?" said Mrs. Kane, craning her neck to see the climb ahead. "We can eat rocks."

Dorothy laughed and helped her mother onto the long boulder. Mr. Kane stood up and stretched. "Let's get going," he said.

"No fair!" said Mrs. Kane. "I just got here!"

But Mr. Kane bounded up the final hill like a mountain goat, and Chloe and Harry followed.

"Who does he think he is, Bambi?" said her mother as Dorothy pulled her to her feet and dragged her up the slope.

They finally reached the top, and Mrs. Kane collapsed in a heap. "Henry," she said. "You'll have to find another way down." Dorothy knew that she was serious, because she usually called her father Hank. Henry meant business.

Mr. Kane went scouting as they unpacked the knapsack and started eating lunch.

"I'm starving," said Harry, wolfing down a peanut butter and jelly sandwich.

"That's because it's almost three o'clock!" said Mrs. Kane.

Mr. Kane reappeared and took a sandwich for himself. "There are some markers at the other end. It will take us a little longer, but we can go down the other side of the mountain."

"Thank goodness," said Mrs. Kane. Dorothy

50

was relieved, too. It was a lot easier being an ac- tress than a mountain guide.

"I'm so sorry, children," said Dorothy's mother. "I haven't set a very good example."

"That's okay," said Harry. "It's kind of neat doing something better than you."

Mrs. Kane laughed and passed out juice boxes. "You're the greatest," she said.

It was better going down. The trail wandered a little, but Dorothy and Harry scouted for markers, which were red this time.

And then the markers disappeared.

"Should we go back, Henry?" said Mrs. Kane in a low voice.

Mr. Kane squinted at his watch. "I'm afraid to," he said. "It'll be getting dark out soon."

He looked as if he knew where he was going. It never occurred to Dorothy that he was pre- tending, because he parted bushes expertly, and skirted trees, and wound in and out of forests and up and down hills, until Dorothy spoke up.

"I think we were here before," she said.

"She's right," said Chloe. "I remember that funny tree that looks like an old lady."

"I remember it, too," Harry chimed in. "We're lost!"

"Did you pack a compass?" asked Chloe, who learned about that kind of thing in the third grade. "Can we find the North Star or something?"

Mr. Kane looked almost as upset as he did when he discovered Dorothy's poison ivy. He didn't answer Chloe.

"We have flashlights!" said Dorothy, looking up at the darkening sky.

Mr. Kane fished in his knapsack for the two flashlights and handed one to Mrs. Kane without speaking.

Dorothy rubbed the goose bumps on her arms. It was getting cold out, too, but she didn't tell her father. He looked worried enough.

Dorothy's mother noticed. "The children don't have any sweaters, Hank. What are we going to do?" She handed her flashlight to Dorothy as she bent to tie her sneaker.

Dorothy pretended she was holding a search-light and circled the woods slowly with it. She didn't know what she was looking for—a sign, a marker, anything—when it flashed on something that glinted like metal. "What's that?" she said to her mother.

Mrs. Kane moved the beam of light along the object. "It's a water pipe," she said. "Henry, isn't that a water pipe?"

"It certainly is!" said Mr. Kane. He sounded excited.

"What's so good about that?" said Harry.

"It could lead down to a road," said Mr. Kane. "Your sister may have saved us!"

Dorothy was instantly a mountain guide again. They followed the water pipe wherever it went, skirting around any overgrown bushes that covered it until they found the pipe again.

"Let's hope it doesn't go underground," Dorothy heard her mother say.

Nobody complained that they were tired or cold, or that their feet hurt. They just kept walking. Suddenly, Mr. Kane shouted, "Stop!" He pointed the flashlight several feet ahead of him. There was a road.

"Hurray!" shouted Harry, jumping up and down.

"We did it!" shouted Dorothy, giving Chloe a hug.

"*You* did it!" said her father, grabbing Dorothy and lifting her up in the air.

It was an empty road. They walked and walked, watching for a sign of headlights in the distance.

"I hear a car!" said Chloe, and they all stopped in their tracks and listened.

It was a station wagon, and it didn't slow down until it was almost next to them. First Mr. Kane, then Harry, then Chloe, then Dorothy, and then Dorothy's mother stuck out their thumbs as if they were hitchhikers.

"Stop!" shouted Dorothy in a voice that would carry across the largest theater.

And the station wagon stopped.

The car seat felt wonderful, even if Harry had

to sit on his mother's lap and Dorothy had to sit on her father's lap, and Chloe was wedged in between.

"What are you folks doing out here in the middle of the night?" said the man driving the car.

"We would have passed you if we hadn't heard the little girl call," said his wife.

"We got lost," said Mr. Kane, kissing Dorothy on the head.

When they finally reached their cabin, the rickety cots never felt so good. Dorothy snuggled into the rough woolen blanket, and it felt just as cozy as the new blue quilt with the pigs on it.

"You were all troupers," said her mother as she kissed them good-night. "You must be very proud of yourself," she whispered to Dorothy.

Dorothy's eyes were already closed. She thought for a moment. She had survived poison ivy and the first week at her new school. She had made a new friend. And who knows? Maybe they would all be sleeping in the woods this very minute if she hadn't found the water pipe.

Dorothy opened her eyes. "Mama?" she called.

"Yes, dear?" said her mother, tiptoeing over.

"I'm very proud," said Dorothy. "But I think I'd rather be an actress than a mountain guide." And she fell asleep.

4

Starring Dorothy Kane

AFTER SCHOOL ON Monday, Jessica came home with Dorothy to play.

"Oh," said Jessica when they entered Dorothy's new bedroom. "I thought maybe you'd have bunk beds or something."

"I have my own room now," said Dorothy proudly. "I used to share with my brother, Harry."

"It must have been nice having somebody to talk to at night," said Jessica, sitting on Dorothy's blue pig quilt. "I don't have any brothers or sisters."

"You're lucky," said Dorothy. "Nobody listens to me anyway." Dorothy brightened. "Except on our trip, when we got lost in the woods. Would you like to hear about it?"

"Sure," said Jessica, watching as Dorothy stepped up onto her wooden toy box.

Dorothy took a deep breath and clasped her hands in front of her. She remembered that awful day in the classroom when she and Jessica had to stand up and speak. For an instant, the words froze in her throat, but Jessica looked so friendly sitting on her bed with Dorothy's new pig-shaped pillow on her lap.

"Go ahead!" her friend urged.

Dorothy took another deep breath and, in a clear voice, began telling her story. . . .

"It was getting darker and darker and darker," continued Dorothy. "We walked and walked and

58

walked. Suddenly . . ." Dorothy opened her eyes wide and spoke so low that Jessica had to lean forward on the bed to hear her. "I said to my father, 'We were here before!' My father looked very scared and so did my mother. I took my mother's flashlight and looked into the woods. There were terrible noises!" Dorothy stopped.

Jessica took a deep breath. "And what happened?" she said. "This is much better than anything on television!"

"I saw a bear! At least, I thought I did, but it turned out to be Harry, leaning against a tree. Suddenly, I found something. . . . My father told me later that it saved our lives."

"What?" asked Jessica, clasping the pig pillow to her. "Tell me!"

"It was a metal pipe!" said Dorothy, but when she saw Jessica's disappointed face, she added, "It looked like a gigantic boa constrictor at first!"

That seemed to satisfy Jessica, and when Dorothy finished the rest of the story, Jessica clapped loudly. Dorothy remembered watching the actors bow in the Cinderella play her mother took her to see, and she copied them exactly.

Dorothy rummaged in her dress-up drawer and pulled out a pair of her mother's old high heels. "We can act out the story," she said to Jessica. "You can be my mother and Chloe and Harry, and I'll be the rest."

"Okay," said Jessica, looking doubtful as she took off her shoes and put on the high heels. "Does your mother really wear these when she hikes?"

"Of course not," said Dorothy. She didn't tell Jessica that her mother only wore them to parties and that the rest of the time she wore sneakers. "You can wear them in the cabin," she said. "And we can bring a baby on the hike, and make believe that the baby is almost eaten by bears!"

"And the mother saves the baby?" said Jessica excitedly.

Dorothy shook her head. "I save the baby," she said, but Jessica's mouth was turning down at the edges, and Dorothy said, "We can take turns."

They played getting lost in the woods for the rest of the afternoon. Mrs. Kane knocked on the door and invited Jessica to stay for dinner.

"We're having spaghetti," Dorothy whispered in Jessica's ear.

"Yes, please," said Jessica. "From a can, like my mother's?"

Mrs. Kane laughed. "From a box," she said. "I'll go call your mother."

Jessica and Dorothy sat next to each other at dinner. They twirled their spaghetti and put it in their mouths at the same time. They ate raspberry Jell-o with whipped cream, and when Dorothy took a spoonful, so did Jessica. They both said *mmm* together.

"Dorothy told me about getting lost in the woods," said Jessica. "I heard about the noises and thinking they were bears, but it turned out to be Harry."

"It did?" said Harry, licking the whipped cream off his spoon.

"What noises?" said Chloe.

"I heard about Dorothy saving everybody by finding the metal pipe," said Jessica.

"That's very true," said Mr. Kane.

"And how she saved everybody from getting poison ivy because she was the only one who knew what it looked like," added Jessica.

"Some of it I made up, to make it more exciting," said Dorothy quickly.

"Dorothy is an excellent storyteller," said Mrs. Kane, smiling.

"She's going to be an actress when she grows up," said Chloe.

"Maybe," said Dorothy, remembering the butterflies in her stomach when she had to stand up in class. "Is there any more Jell-o?" she asked her mother, changing the subject. The second helping of Jell-o was just as good as the first . . . but it didn't make her forget about the butterflies.

The next day at school, Mrs. Greenaway wrote on the blackboard: "Tell a story, recite a poem." First they talked about different kinds of poetry.

Mrs. Greenaway read them a limerick. She read them a sonnet by Shakespeare. She read them a few of her favorite Mother Goose rhymes.

"Starting tomorrow," said Mrs. Greenaway, "I'd like each of you to tell a story or recite a poem that you know, in front of the class."

Some of the children groaned loudly. Dorothy was one of them.

"What's the matter?" whispered Jessica. "You'll do great! Would you like to practice at my house after school?"

"I guess so," said Dorothy, getting that funny feeling in her stomach again. At lunchtime, she couldn't eat the turkey sandwich or the two double-dipped Oreo cookies that her mother had packed for her.

After school, Dorothy asked her mother if she could go to Jessica's house.

"My mother's picking me up," explained Jessica. "But sometimes she's late. She gets caught up in things."

"I'll wait with you until she comes," said Mrs. Kane.

At last Jessica's mother came running into the school yard. Her hair was tied back with a colorful scarf, and there was a smudge of green paint on her cheek.

"Sorry," she gasped, brushing back strands of her hair with a hand full of purple and pink paint. "I started work on a new painting, and the sky is giving me a bit of trouble."

"My mother is a painter," Jessica said proudly. "This is my friend, Dorothy," she added, putting an arm around her.

"I'm glad to meet you," said Jessica's mother. "I'm Rikki Brothers. I've heard so much about you."

"Are you painting a sunset?" asked Dorothy, looking at the different colors on Mrs. Brothers's hand.

"Not necessarily," said Jessica's mother, smiling. "Jessica tells me you're going to be an actress when you grow up."

"She's better than 'Sesame Street,'" said Jessica.

"But not better than Teenage Mutant Ninja Turtles," said Harry, yanking on his mother's hand.

"I'll come and get Dorothy later," Mrs. Kane called after them as Harry pulled her down the street. "My son is pretending he's a dog on a leash."

"Woof, woof," barked Harry.

"That means good-bye," said Dorothy, laughing as she waved to him.

"It must be nice having a brother," said Jessica.

Jessica's house was like her mother—colorful and messy. The walls of the kitchen were painted red, and there was a painted rainbow above the kitchen table. Mrs. Brothers made them fruit salad faces for a snack: melon eyes, a raisin smile, a grape for a nose, and pineapple chunks for the hair.

"This is great," said Dorothy, until Jessica asked her what poem she was going to recite. Dorothy took her raisin mouth and arranged it so that it frowned. The bad feeling was back in her stomach.

They finished up their fruit faces and went upstairs to Jessica's room. Jessica cleared some toys off her bed, which was covered by a bright patchwork quilt. The walls were decorated with black handprints and footprints of every shape and size.

"I like your wallpaper," said Dorothy.

"Oh, that's not wallpaper, that's my hands and feet. Mom had me step in black paint, and then we printed my footprints on the wall. We did it every few months."

"It must be nice, being the only kid in the house," said Dorothy. Her mother read them lots of books and did lots of loads of laundry. But Dorothy couldn't imagine making footprints with her every few months.

Jessica shrugged and pushed some stuffed animals off a wooden toy chest which also had handprints on it. "We got carried away!" she said. Then Jessica stepped up on the box and announced, "This can be the stage. I'll go first."

Jessica stood for a moment. Her face looked blank. Then she said, "'I'm a Little Teapot'?" and frowned. "Too boring?"

"It might be too short," said Dorothy. She tried to think of a good poem. "Mary Had a Little Lamb" was very babyish, and anyway, there were too many verses. "Little Bo-Peep" was much too dumb—she was always losing her sheep. "The Old Woman Who Lived in a Shoe" not only spanked her kids, but she put them to bed without any supper. Dorothy's parents would never do that. They'd make her sit in her room and call it time out. "Georgie Porgie" was no good—it would make the boys laugh when she mentioned the kissing.

"I can't think of anything," said Dorothy, sighing loudly.

"'I'm a Little Teapot' is stupid," said Jessica, looking as dejected as Dorothy. Suddenly, she jumped down off the toy chest and ran over to her bookshelf. "My old nursery rhyme book!"

she said triumphantly. They sat down together and looked through the pictures. They were happy that they knew most of the poems by heart, so they wouldn't have to memorize anything new.

Jessica found a short one. "You go first," she said to Dorothy. "I'll watch how you do it, because you're the actress."

Dorothy wished Jessica had never heard that she wanted to be an actress. She was beginning to feel queasy. She leafed through the rest of the book and chose "The Queen of Hearts." Maybe it wasn't too dumb. She stepped up on the box. Her heart began to beat quickly. She could see the huge classroom full of children. All of them were looking at her.

"Go ahead," said Jessica in an encouraging voice.

Dorothy took a deep breath and started to recite. Halfway through the poem, she stopped. She looked at Jessica's face. There was no doubt about it. Her friend looked bored.

"Let me start over," said Dorothy. Dorothy fixed an imaginary crown on her head and pretended she was rolling out some dough. Then she said, "'The queen of hearts, she made some tarts, all on a summer's day.'" Dorothy wiped some imaginary sweat off her forehead. Then she made believe she was a thief, looking every which way with her eyes narrowed, and she grabbed an imaginary tray of tarts. "'The knave of hearts,'" she said, thumping on her heart, "'he stole those tarts, and took them clean away.'"

When Dorothy had finished, Jessica clapped loudly. "That was great!" said Jessica. "Now it's my turn." She took Dorothy's place on the wooden box, and started to recite, "'To market, to market, to buy a plum bun.'" Then she stopped. "Too squeaky?" she said in a worried voice.

"It's fine," said Dorothy. "Just keep your voice low."

Jessica finished her poem, and the girls shook hands. They still had time to play their lost-in-

69

the-woods game, and then the doorbell rang and it was time for Dorothy to go home.

That night, Dorothy couldn't sleep. She read some books under her covers with a flashlight. She played with two of her Barbie dolls. She sang a little. Nothing helped. When she read, all she could think about was "The Queen of Hearts." She had one of her Barbie dolls recite it. And when she sang, it was "The Queen of Hearts," over and over, until her mother knocked on the door and said, "Bedtime, young lady!"

Mrs. Kane took one look at Dorothy's face in the morning and served her cinnamon toast. That was Dorothy's favorite breakfast treat, even if it was on whole-wheat bread. But the cinnamon toast didn't get rid of the butterflies in Dorothy's stomach. Only half a piece got eaten, and she left for school feeling like it was her first day, and horrible, all over again.

At school, Dorothy's heart was beating so loudly that she leaned over and asked Jessica if she could hear it.

"Of course not," said Jessica, laughing.

Mrs. Greenaway was talking about the weather, and wrote the words "cool and breezy" on the blackboard. Dorothy was glad that the teacher hadn't asked her what she thought the weather was like, because she couldn't even remember. She had been reciting "The Queen of Hearts" since she left the house in the morning. Now Mrs. Greenaway was talking about what kinds of things happened in the month of October. Dorothy heard someone call out, "Halloween!" Somebody else said, "The leaves change colors." If Mrs. Greenaway had asked her, Dorothy would have answered "'The knave of hearts, he stole some tarts,'" even if it was on a summer's day and not in October.

At last, the teacher looked at a list and said, "Joshua, how about telling us a story or reciting a poem?"

Joshua stood up, and Mrs. Greenaway motioned for him to come to the front of the classroom. He clasped his hands tightly in front of him. Dorothy thought his face looked even paler than usual against his red hair. Joshua cleared his throat, and Dorothy's heart started racing.

"I'm going to tell a story about my little brother. He was coughing a lot," said Joshua. His voice sounded loud to Dorothy in the quiet classroom. "Anyway, a few days ago my mother went into his room to check on him. She does that a lot. And she started screaming for my father. Really loud, which is funny for my mom, because she's pretty quiet." Joshua's face was pinker now, and he started motioning with his hands. "My dad ran into the room and scooped up the baby like he was a football or something. My mother grabbed me by the arm and dragged me out of the house, and I knew something was really wrong, because she didn't even make me put on my coat."

Joshua paused, and Dorothy leaned forward eagerly in her seat to hear what happened. "In fact, I didn't even have my coat with me. I remember it was kind of cold out. Anyway, we jumped into the car, and I put on my seat belt even though I usually wait for my mom to tell me. 'Step on it!' my mother shouted to my dad, and he drove like he was a race car driver or something. We even went through a yellow light, and my dad always slows down for them." Joshua stopped abruptly. Then he said, "I was going to do 'Jack and Jill Went Up the Hill,' but I changed my mind. Too dumb."

"And we're glad you did, Joshua," said Mrs. Greenaway. "But what happened?" She sounded excited.

"Oh," said Joshua, with a smile on his face. "We got to the hospital, and my dad didn't even park the car. He just pulled into this part that said NO PARKING. We all jumped out of the car, and the baby was making these awful growling noises and my mom had this scared look on her face. A nurse came over and took the baby, and I stayed with my dad while we told somebody how old the baby was and what address we lived at. And that's the end of the story."

Some of the children started calling out,

"What happened to the baby?" and Mrs. Greenaway held out her hands and said, "Quiet down, class." Then she turned to Joshua, who was walking back to his seat, and said, "You see, Joshua, you told that story so well that we need to know more. Is the baby all right?"

Joshua looked surprised. "Oh, yeah," he said. "It was something called the croup, and he stayed overnight at the hospital and my parents took him home the next day."

"That was excellent," said Mrs. Greenaway, consulting her list again. "Jessica Brothers. Will you go next, please?"

Jessica walked to the front of the room. Dorothy held her breath and wondered if Jessica would get scared and start squeaking like she did on the second day of school.

Jessica's arms dangled at her sides. She looked down at them as if they didn't belong to her, and she fished in her dress for some pockets to hide them in. When she discovered that her dress *had* no pockets, she clasped them behind her. She began speaking.

"'To market, to market, to buy a plum bun. Home again, home again, market is done.'" Her voice was very faint, but she didn't squeak. Jessica took a deep breath and started on the second stanza. "'To market, to market, to buy a fat pig—'"

"Like Benny Spignolli!" somebody shouted.

"Stop that at once!" Mrs. Greenaway said sternly, and before she could say any more, Jessica added, "'Home again, home again, jiggedy jig,'" and ran to her seat.

"Well done," said Mrs. Greenaway. "Even with the rude interruption." She looked at her list again. "Andrea? Are you ready?"

Andrea spoke so quickly that it took Dorothy a moment to realize what she was reciting. Dorothy's heart sank. It was "The Queen of Hearts." She chanted every verse and sat down.

"A little fast," said Mrs. Greenaway, "but very nice. Dorothy? Can we hear your poem or story?"

Dorothy stared at the scratches on her wooden desk. Her face felt hot and sweaty. Maybe Mrs.

Greenaway would think she had a fever. Maybe she *did* have a fever, and the teacher would have to send her home. Dorothy wiped her hand across her forehead, but Mrs. Greenaway didn't get the hint.

"Dorothy?" she said firmly.

Dorothy walked to the front of the classroom. She felt like the lady in an old movie her father had watched, about a spy who got shot by a firing squad. They blindfolded her and made her stand in front of all these people. Dorothy's mother said it wasn't suitable for children and made her leave the room, but she heard the shot anyway.

Dorothy stood awkwardly, shifting her feet from side to side. Her eyes wandered around the classroom. Benny Spignolli was slouching in his seat, chewing on something. He looked like he was ready to throw a spitball. Maybe she was standing in front of a spitball squad but without a blindfold. Benny looked at Dorothy and made a sound like a frog, but he didn't throw anything.

Dorothy quickly fixed her eyes on Jessica, whose face looked stricken. She cleared her throat, and it felt like sandpaper. She swallowed, and it sounded very loud to her. Her heart felt like it was beating in her head. She cleared her throat for the second time, and through the thumping in her head she heard Jessica say, "Tell them about getting lost in the woods."

Dorothy's head started to clear a little, and she said in a tiny voice, "The whole family went for a walk in the woods." She looked at Jessica, who was nodding her head. Dorothy pictured herself back in her bedroom on her wooden box, telling Jessica the story for the very first time. Jessica was smiling now, and Dorothy's voice grew stronger. When she got to the part about the noises in the woods turning out to be Harry, Benny Spignolli called out, "He thought he was in the second grade again." Everybody started laughing. Dorothy froze, and then she said quickly, "Suddenly, a *real* bear jumped out of the bushes, and we all thought he was Benny Spignolli, and it scared us to death!" The children started laughing hysterically, and Dorothy held out her hands and imitated Mrs. Greenaway when she wanted them to quiet down.

"And when I crawled into bed, I didn't worry about bugs or mice or anything. I just pulled my covers up to my chin, and like Dorothy in *The Wizard of Oz* . . ." Dorothy finished her story with a flourish. ". . . There was no place like home."

Dorothy sat down quickly. Her heart was still hammering, but it was hammering because of all the clapping she heard around her. Her cheeks were bright pink, but they were pink with happiness.

"We'll hear some more speakers later," said Mrs. Greenaway, folding up her list. "That was terrific, Dorothy."

"Better than anything on television," Jessica said out loud.

"There aren't any bears in the woods around here," said Benny Spignolli.

"You were almost as good as me," said Joshua.

"Not as boring as my poem," said Andrea.

And Dorothy had to agree. And it didn't matter that Benny Spignolli was right about the bears. After all, an actress had to keep her audience interested, or the play wouldn't go on.

5

Class Trip

WHEN MRS. GREENAWAY told Dorothy's class that they were going on a class trip, everybody cheered. It was fun getting out of the classroom. It was exciting going on a strange bus ride with a lunch box full of goodies. It was great getting out of school.

Mrs. Greenaway passed out permission forms for the children to bring home.

"Have a parent or guardian sign the form, and bring it back as soon as possible," said the teacher.

Andrea raised her hand. "Where are we going?" she said.

"To McDonald's?" called out Benny, who loved hamburgers.

"To the zoo?" shouted George, who had a menagerie of animals in his bedroom, including gerbils, a hamster, a rabbit, and two cats.

"To a play?" cried Dorothy.

Mrs. Greenaway smiled and shook her head. "If you'll give me a chance, I'll tell you. Do you remember how we talked about families during the first week of school? And some of you were lucky enough to have grandparents and even great-grandparents still alive?"

Dorothy remembered, because that was when her stage fright first began. But what kind of class trip involved your grandma and grandpa? Certainly not a trip to a play, or a zoo, or McDonald's, even if Grandma Rebecca *did* like their french fries.

Mrs. Greenaway continued. "We'll be visiting a nursing home called the Happy Springs Home for the Aged, where my mother happens to be staying."

Some of the children groaned, but not Dorothy. She thought that Mrs. Greenaway might not like it if she made a rude noise at the mention of visiting her mother. But looking at Mrs. Greenaway's face, which had more wrinkles on it than Dorothy's mother's, and looking at her hair, which was almost all gray, Dorothy couldn't help wondering how old Mrs. Greenaway's mother might be. She must be ancient!

That evening, Dorothy gave her mother the permission slip to sign.

"If you don't want me to go, it's okay," said Dorothy.

Mrs. Kane smiled. She squinted slightly as she read the slip of paper, and Dorothy could see the little crow's feet in the corners of her mother's eyes.

"When you get older," said Dorothy, "will

you go into a nursing home like Great-Grandma Fanny?"

Mrs. Kane took a minute to answer. "It depends," she said. "Hopefully Daddy and I will keep each other company in our old age."

"I'll keep you company," said Dorothy fiercely. "I won't ever leave."

"Not for a long time," said Mrs. Kane. "But some day you will. As for Great-Grandma Fanny, she was just too sick to live by herself anymore."

Dorothy thought for a moment. "Are Grandpa Leon and Grandma Rebecca going to get sick and go and live in a nursing home?"

"Let's hope not," said Mrs. Kane, and she took her pen and signed the form.

Even though it was only a trip to a nursing home, there was an air of excitement as Dorothy stepped onto the big yellow bus. Her only disappointment was that they had already eaten lunch so there would be no lunch box goodies, but at least she got to sit next to Jessica on the bus.

Dorothy and Jessica held hands as they walked into the nursing home. There was a desk with a sign above it that said RECEPTION, and Mrs. Greenaway spoke to a lady there. Some old people were sitting on green plastic chairs, others on mustard yellow couches. Dorothy saw a lady with two white braids sitting next to a man with a mop of wavy white hair. They were holding hands.

Benny Spignolli and Marcus Elliott saw them, too, because they started laughing and pointing. Dorothy was glad that the old people didn't seem to notice.

"I wonder which one is Mrs. Greenaway's mother," Dorothy whispered to Jessica.

"I'll bet it's her," said Jessica, nodding her head toward a lady who was reading a book. "Mrs. Greenaway says reading is the most important skill we can learn, and that lady looks like she loves to read."

"She has a chin like Mrs. Greenaway's, too," agreed Dorothy. "Kind of pointy."

"Then again," said Jessica, looking around the big room, "that one over there is reading, too."

"And she has a mole on her cheek that looks like Mrs. Greenaway's," said Dorothy.

"You're right," said Jessica. "With hairs in it."

Dorothy covered her mouth to keep from giggling. Somehow the nursing home reminded her of a museum or a library . . . a place where you weren't supposed to laugh.

Benny and Marcus didn't think so. Benny pointed to the old lady with a mole on her cheek and whispered loudly, "That one looks like she's ready to take off on her broomstick!"

Marcus laughed so loudly that he made snorting noises, but Mrs. Greenaway caught his eye and gave him a very icy stare, and Marcus stopped.

It turned out that neither one of the old ladies was Mrs. Greenaway's mother, because the children left the big room and waited for the elevator to take them to the second floor. Joshua's mother took half the class, herding them into the elevator with "Come, little ones," and Mrs. Greenaway took the other half, including Dorothy and Jessica. Dorothy was glad, because Joshua's mother talked to the children as if they were a bunch of two-year-olds.

"This is the recreation room," said Mrs. Greenaway as they stepped out of the elevator and entered a brightly decorated yellow room with several people crowded around a television set. They were watching what Dorothy's father called a dope opera instead of a soap opera. Dorothy's mother sometimes watched the tail end of "General Hospital" after picking up the children from school, but not like the people in the nursing home. Their eyes were glued to the set, and only two of the ladies looked up when the children approached. Dorothy's mother laughed a lot more and switched it off when Harry or Dorothy wanted to watch cartoons.

Mrs. Greenaway was talking to a younger lady with a ponytail, and the lady walked over to the television set and turned it off.

"Hey, I was watching that!" said an old man with a head shaped like an egg and just as bald.

"We have some special guests, Mr. Greenspan, and I know you'll want to meet them," said the lady with the ponytail.

"Who says?" said the old man, scratching his egg-shaped head. "I never asked to meet them."

Dorothy had never heard a grown-up speak so rudely before, but the lady with the ponytail didn't seem to mind.

"They're going to sing us some songs," continued the lady, "and I know you'll all give them a big welcome."

Some of the old people clapped. Dorothy and her class lined up to sing, but not before Dorothy heard the old man say, "If I wanted music, I could turn on the radio."

At last Mrs. Greenaway announced the last song. "We're going to sing a traditional Thanksgiving song, although Thanksgiving is still a few weeks away," she said.

"First there's Halloween and candy!" shouted

Benny Spignolli, who liked candy as much as he liked hamburgers.

One of the old ladies laughed and said, "He reminds me of my son. He likes his food, too."

"Halloween is next week," said Mrs. Greenaway, smiling, "And that means Thanksgiving is just around the corner. So here we go." She lifted up her hands like a conductor, and the class began singing, "'Over the river and through the woods, to grandmother's house we go.'"

When they had finished, the old people clapped very loudly. Dorothy saw one of them take out a handkerchief and wipe away a tear. Joshua's mother asked Dorothy and Joshua to help pass out cookies that she had baked, and Dorothy went directly to the old lady. Maybe if she pretended she was a nurse, like Florence Nightingale, she could make the old lady feel better.

"Would you like one?" she said. "They're chocolate chip."

"I would love one," said the old lady, sighing

the way Dorothy's grandma sometimes did as she took a cookie. "That song reminded me of all the Thanksgivings I used to make for my family."

"Won't they be coming to get you for Thanksgiving?" said Dorothy hopefully.

"I suppose so," said the old lady, biting into her cookie. "My daughter prepares the whole thing."

"I'll bet she's a good cook," said Dorothy, in her best Florence Nightingale voice.

"She is," said the old lady. "But I'm even better!" she added with a laugh.

Dorothy left the old lady smiling and walked over to the man with the egg head. Maybe a cookie would put him in a better mood, too. If Harry was grouchy, it sometimes helped. She held the cookie plate out to him, hoping he wouldn't knock it out of her hand.

"Would you like one?" said Dorothy in a small voice.

The old man sniffed at the cookies. "Are they any good?" he said.

"I don't know," said Dorothy. "I haven't tried one."

"So try one," said the old man, "and let me know."

Dorothy looked around. Some of the children were sitting on the couch, eating cookies. Benny Spignolli had three in one hand. Dorothy selected the cookie with the most chocolate chips in it and took a bite.

"It's delicious," she said. "Maybe it will cheer you up. It always works for my brother Harry."

The old man looked surprised and held out his hand. "Pick a good one for me," he said.

Dorothy selected another chip-filled cookie and placed it in the old man's hand. She watched him take a bite. A big smile appeared on his face. "You pick good cookies," he said. "Your brother Harry is very lucky."

"Oh, he would never ever let me pick for him!" said Dorothy. "He's five years old, and he thinks he's grown-up."

The old man laughed, and Dorothy could see

his stomach go up and down. *"Shainele,"* he said.

"My grandma sometimes calls me that," said Dorothy. "She says it means 'little beauty.'"

"And what's your grandmother's name?" asked the old man, eating the rest of his cookie with relish.

"Rebecca," said Dorothy. "Grandma Rebecca."

The old man's eyes filled with tears, and he rubbed at them with closed fists, kind of like her brother Harry did when he cried.

"I'm sorry," said Dorothy. "Did I say something wrong?"

The old man waved a hand in the air and said, "That was my wife's name. Rebecca. I miss her like you can't imagine."

Mrs. Greenaway was beckoning from the other side of the room, and Dorothy ran over to her.

"Could my mother have a cookie?" she said cheerfully, pointing to a very old lady in a wheel-

91

chair, whose head was cocked to one side. Her hand moved slowly through the air and hovered over the cookie plate, and the old lady's wrist was so thin that it looked like a chicken bone. She lowered the hand and reached for a cookie. Then she chewed off the smallest crumb and held the rest of the cookie in her hand.

"Is that good, Mother?" said Mrs. Greenaway.

The old lady didn't answer. She moved her mouth some more, as if she were chewing, but Dorothy knew that she must have finished the tiny bite she had taken.

Mrs. Greenaway took the cookie and wrapped it in a napkin. "Maybe you'll eat it later, Mother," she said, tucking it into the old lady's pocket.

"It's very good," said Dorothy, looking across the room to see if the old man with the egg head was still crying. She was glad to see the lady with the ponytail standing next to him, with her hand on his shoulder.

"Time for us to go!" announced Mrs. Greenaway, and she kissed her mother on the cheek. "Buddies, please," she called to the children, and Dorothy looked around for Jessica. There was a tap on her shoulder, and the lady with the pony-tail said to Dorothy, "Mr. Greenspan would like to say good-bye to you."

Dorothy walked over to the man with the egg head. He was holding his arms out like he was her grandfather, and Dorothy gave him a hug. She was glad he wasn't crying anymore.

"Good-bye, *shainele*," said the old man. "Thank you for visiting."

"Good-bye, Mr. Greenspan," said Dorothy, wondering why he was thanking her when she had made him cry.

The lady with the ponytail was next to her again, and she walked Dorothy over to the rest of the children. "That's the first time Mr. Greenspan has cried since his wife died," she said.

"I'm sorry," said Dorothy, alarmed.

"We're very grateful, honey," said the lady

93

gently, patting Dorothy on the shoulder.

Dorothy didn't tell Jessica about making the old man with the egg head cry. She didn't tell her teacher when she helped all the children off the bus, or Joshua's mother when she gave Dorothy a wet kiss and thanked her for handing out cookies.

Dorothy was glad to see her mother when she picked her up at school. She was even glad to see Harry. They walked home, and Mrs. Kane prepared a snack for them.

"Did the people enjoy your singing?" said Mrs. Kane, pouring Dorothy and Harry glasses of milk at the kitchen table.

"I guess so," said Dorothy. "They clapped a lot."

"Was the home nice?" said Mrs. Kane, deftly slicing an apple and sprinkling the pieces with cinnamon.

"It's not a home," said Dorothy, reaching for a piece. "It's sadder than a home." She chewed the apple slowly and added, "They liked Joshua's mother's cookies. I helped give them out."

"That was nice of you." Mrs. Kane sipped a cup of tea and turned her attention to Harry. "Eat the skin, too, Harry. It's good for you."

"It's gross," said Harry as he continued to spit the apple skin out.

"Benny and Marcus made fun of the old people," said Dorothy, pushing Harry's plate full of apple skin away from her.

"Maybe they don't have grandparents who love them the way you do," said Dorothy's mother.

"I don't think anyone could love Benny Spignolli," said Dorothy, laughing.

"I'm sure his mother does, in her own way," said Mrs. Kane, but she started laughing, too.

"And his gross brother," said Harry, arranging his apple peel in a pile.

"Mrs. Greenaway's mother isn't like a real mother," said Dorothy. "She's worse than . . . Harry."

"What's the matter with me?" said Harry,

spitting out another piece of apple peel.

"She's like a baby," said Dorothy. "Mrs. Greenaway practically feeds her."

"Nobody feeds me!" said Harry, gulping down his milk.

"You're very grown-up," said Mrs. Kane, smoothing the top of Harry's head. "It's hard when your parents get old," she said to Dorothy. "Then the children have to be the parents."

"If I was your parent," said Harry, "I'd let you have ice cream for every meal."

"Then I guess I'd have to eat it," said Mrs. Kane, laughing. "Until then, eat your apple peel."

"Two of the old people cried," said Dorothy, watching her mother's face. "An old man cried when I told him about Grandma Rebecca, and Rebecca was his wife's name, and she just died."

"You're not supposed to make people cry," said Harry. "That's why I had to give Benjamin his boat back."

"The lady with the ponytail said she was

glad," said Dorothy hotly. "And when he hugged me good-bye, he looked happy. Isn't that weird?"

"You're weird!" said Harry, singing, "Dorothy made a man cry, Dorothy made a man cry!"

"Hush, Harry!" said Mrs. Kane, rubbing a finger across Dorothy's cheek. "There are all kinds of crying," she said. "We're lucky, because we haven't lost anyone who is dear to us. But when someone dies, you have to mourn the person who has left you. That's how you helped the old man."

"Crying made him feel better?" said Dorothy.

"Yes," said Mrs. Kane.

"But you don't like it when Harry cries if you won't let him watch his cartoons," said Dorothy.

"Or when Dorothy cries and whines for a dumb new Barbie doll," said Harry, poking Dorothy in the side.

"No hitting," said Mrs. Kane, but it looked as if she was trying to keep from smiling. "As I said—there are all different kinds of crying."

"Did Daddy cry when Grandpa Harry died?" asked Dorothy.

"He cried like a baby," said Mrs. Kane.

"When you die, I'll cry a lot, too," said Harry, grabbing his Super Ball and running out of the room. "Or I'll come with you!" he shouted from the other room.

Mrs. Kane put down her teacup so quickly that it clinked loudly against the saucer.

"He can't come with you, can he?" said Dorothy.

"No, dear," her mother said gently. "He can't."

"And I really made the old man feel better?" said Dorothy.

"I'm sure you did," said Mrs. Kane.

Dorothy stood up from the kitchen table. "Can I call Grandma?" she asked.

"Of course," said her mother. She dialed the number and handed her the receiver.

"Grandma Rebecca?" said Dorothy when her grandmother answered.

"*Shainele,*" said Grandma. "How's my granddaughter?"

"I met an old man who called me that," said Dorothy. "*Shainele,* just like you do." She could hear her grandmother tell her grandfather, "Dorothy's on the phone!"

"So where did you meet this old man?" said Grandma. "Your grandpa will get jealous."

"We met him on a class trip. He reminded me a little of Grandpa, only Grandpa has more hair." Dorothy waited until her grandmother stopped laughing. Then she said, "I love you, Grandma. And tell Grandpa that I love him, too."

When Dorothy hung up the phone, she looked over at her mother, who was still sipping the same cup of tea. A tear was glistening in the corner of her mother's eye, and it slid down her cheek.

"That's a different kind of crying, isn't it, Mama?" said Dorothy.

"Yes," said her mother, smiling.

6

A Visit to
Grandma's Condominium

WHEN DOROTHY'S MOTHER told her they were taking a trip to Grandma's home in Florida for their winter vacation, Dorothy said, "Can Jessica come with us?"

"Jessica will be celebrating Christmas with *her* family," said Mrs. Kane.

"Is there snow in Florida?" said Harry, who

liked a snowstorm almost as much as he liked vanilla fudge ice cream.

"No," said Mrs. Kane. "But it's nice and hot there, and we can go to the swimming pool every day."

"No, thank you," said Harry. "I'd rather build a snowman."

"We can ride the waves at the beach," said Mr. Kane hopefully.

"I'd rather play in my snow fort," said Harry, parting the curtains to see if it had started snowing yet.

"You can't go ice skating there, either, Harry," said Chloe.

"Thank you, Chloe," said her mother, but Dorothy knew from her tone of voice that she didn't mean it at all.

"We have to go on an airplane to get there, Harry," said Dorothy. She knew because Grandma always talked about the airsick pills that she took before she went on a plane.

"We do?" said Harry, letting go of the curtain.

"You can make believe you're a pilot," said Dorothy.

"I can?" said Harry, flapping his arms out as if he were ready to fly.

"Absolutely," said Mr. Kane, winking at Dorothy. "It's very exciting, going on an airplane."

Harry was interested now. "Is it as scary as a roller coaster?" he said.

"It had better not be," said Chloe. "Or you can count me out."

"Once you take off," said Mrs. Kane hastily, "you hardly know you're in the air." She rolled her eyes at Mr. Kane, because she knew that Chloe could be even stubborner than Harry.

Harry parted the curtains again, but this time it was to watch for airplanes. "Wait until I tell my friends at school," he said.

Harry wore swimming goggles and a helmet on the day of departure. Chloe wore shiny new sunglasses that her mother let her pick out. Dorothy carried a brand new pink plastic pocketbook with a stamped envelope in it, because she had promised that she would write to Jessica. Mrs. Kane took two aspirin, and Mr. Kane hurt his back dragging the suitcases out to the car.

"What have you got in there, my barbells?" he said grumpily to Mrs. Kane, thumping the final suitcase into the trunk.

"Of course not," said Dorothy's mother. "There's an exercise room and a sauna at my mother's condominium."

Mr. Kane stopped grumbling by the time they got to the airport, and Dorothy heard her mother say that the aspirins had begun to work.

They were almost two hours early. While Mrs. Kane sat with the hand luggage, Dorothy and Chloe and Harry visited the gift shop with their father. Mr. Kane told the children that they could pick out one item apiece for the plane ride.

"As long as it's not too expensive," he said.

Dorothy, who was pretending she was a movie star with a pen in her pocketbook all ready to sign autographs, chose a packet of sugarless bubble gum. She felt very grown-up putting it in her purse. She also planned on offering someone a stick of it in the airplane, just the way she had seen her mother do.

Harry chose a Teenage Mutant Ninja Turtle figurine. "I thought you had this one," said Mr. Kane, giving him the money. "They all look alike."

Chloe asked her father if she could buy a magazine called *Teen*. Dorothy noticed that his eyebrows went up into the air, but he gave her a dollar and fifty cents and said, "I guess you can practice your reading with it." Mr. Kane talked as much about reading as Mrs. Greenaway did.

By the time they heard the announcement for Flight 102 to Fort Lauderdale, Harry was complaining that there were snow flurries outside, and maybe they should wait until tomorrow to visit Grandma.

"She'll be waiting for us at the airport," Mrs. Kane reminded him. "And she told me she has a half gallon of vanilla fudge ice cream in the freezer for you, Harry."

Harry shrugged his shoulders and put on his helmet. "I'm ready," he said.

Dorothy was surprised that there were no stairs to climb to get into the plane. They just walked through a covered hallway, the stewardess smiled and took the tickets from Mr. Kane, and they were on the airplane.

The stewardess asked Harry to remove his helmet and put it under his seat.

"But I'm a fighter pilot," complained Harry.

"You're a passenger," said the stewardess, smiling. "But maybe later you can visit the cockpit with me."

Dorothy sat down in the seat next to her mother. Across the aisle, she watched her father pull down his table, and she did the same. He was reading his book already, so Dorothy pulled a sheet out of the envelope addressed to Jessica and took out her new purple felt-tip pen.

She thought for a moment, and then she wrote across the top of the page in her most careful penmanship, *Dear Jessica.* She thought some more and continued writing, *We are on the plane,* concentrating so hard that her tongue stuck out of the corner of her mouth just like Harry's did when he was planning strategies for his Teenage Mutant Ninja Turtles. She wrote the word *love* and signed her name, surrounding it with hearts and stars, the way she thought a movie star would end a letter. Then she put the piece of paper back into the envelope.

"Finished," she said, lifting the flap of the envelope to her mouth to give it a lick.

"Wait a minute," said her mother, snatching the letter from her. "Why don't you see what Florida is like first, and then you can write to Jessica about it?"

"Okay," said Dorothy. She put the envelope back in her purse and pulled out her packet of gum. "Gum, anyone?" she said in her most grown-up movie star voice.

Her mother looked suitably impressed and took one. Harry, who could hear very well now that his helmet was off, shouted across his mother, "I'll have one!"

Dorothy made a face, but she had never seen a grown-up say, "No, you can't have one," unless of course it was a cookie right before dinnertime. She pulled out a stick of gum and ripped it in half. She gave one half to Harry and the other half to Chloe, who was sitting next to her father across the aisle.

"Thank you," said Chloe, lifting up her shiny new sunglasses.

"You look just like an actress," said Dorothy, wondering if she should have chosen sunglasses instead of the pink pocketbook. She turned her attention to the stewardess, who was demonstrating how to put on the oxygen mask and how to use the flotation pillows.

"Are we going to crash?" said Harry loudly. Dorothy felt her heart race like it did when she had stage fright, but her mother said so firmly, "Of course not!" that she felt better immediately.

The plane started to make a very loud noise, worse than Mr. Simpkins's vacuum cleaner at school, and it started to move.

Dorothy held onto the armrests and let her

mother pull the seat belt tighter around her. Chloe took off her sunglasses and sat back in her seat. Mr. Kane kept reading. Harry shouted, "Hurray!" so loudly that Mrs. Kane told him he was disturbing the other passengers, but she smiled and took Harry's hand.

The pilot started talking over the loudspeaker, and Harry put on his goggles and made a very fierce face. "Over and out," he said, over and over until Mrs. Kane had to shush him again so that she could hear what the weather was in Florida.

"Hank!" called Mrs. Kane to her husband.

Mr. Kane put down his book.

"The weather is much cooler today than it said in the paper yesterday," said Mrs. Kane.

"We'll manage," said Mr. Kane, and he turned back to his book. Dorothy heard her mother grumble, "I hope I packed enough warm clothes."

Mrs. Kane looked surprised when the stewardess approached her and said, "I think your little boy rang the buzzer for me."

"Harry?" said Mrs. Kane in amazement.

"I'd like my oxygen mask, please," said Harry in his most serious voice. "I'm experiencing a little dehumidifying now. Over and out."

"We'll have some soft drinks," said Mrs. Kane firmly, but her face was very red. "Sorry," she added, but the stewardess didn't seem to mind, because she winked at Harry and told him he could visit the cockpit as soon as she finished giving out the snacks.

"Hurray!" said Harry. Dorothy started to laugh. Flying with Harry was certainly an adventure. Maybe it would be a good story to tell in class, now that she was going to be an actress again.

The stewardess gave out her final bag of peanuts and beckoned for Harry to follow her to the front of the plane. "Would your sisters like to join you?" she said, turning toward Dorothy.

Dorothy tried scrambling out of her seat until she discovered that she still had on her seat belt. She unhooked herself and tapped on Chloe's shoulder. "Want to go see the pilot?" she said, but Chloe was too busy reading *Teen* magazine to care.

"Wow!" said Harry. "It's much fancier than our computer at school!"

The pilot laughed, and the copilot gave Harry a headset to put on.

"My father wears these when he's jogging," said Harry proudly. "Only they have music in them."

Dorothy tried on the headset next, and she even pressed a button. She would tell her class all about visiting the pilot in the cockpit, too. Even Benny Spignolli would be impressed. Dorothy peered over the pilot's shoulder. She could see a lot more of the sky from the front of the plane, and she hoped the birds knew enough to stay out of the way.

"Would you like to be a pilot when you grow up?" the captain said to Harry.

"No, thank you," said Harry. "I'm going to be a letter carrier like my dad."

"I see," said the captain, and he turned to Dorothy. "How about you? Would you like to be a pilot?"

"I'm going to be an actress," explained Dorothy, but she didn't want the pilot to feel bad, so she added, "Maybe I can act in a movie about Amelia Earhart or something." Dorothy was glad that Mrs. Greenaway had told them about the first woman to fly across the Atlantic, and she was even happier that she had remembered her name.

"And you can fly my airmail over the ocean for me," said Harry.

They said good-bye and returned to their seats, and in no time at all the stewardess announced that they would be landing.

Mrs. Kane fastened their seat belts securely. This time Dorothy chewed on her last piece of gum and looked at the pictures in Chloe's magazine. She wasn't nervous at all.

Then the airplane began to bounce and jump, and Dorothy saw her mother lean forward in her seat and catch her father's eye. Her mother made a scared face and wiped it off as soon as she saw Dorothy watching. Dorothy chewed her gum very quickly and whispered to her mother, "Why are we bouncing around?"

Suddenly, the stewardess announced, "We will be experiencing a bit of turbulence for a while. Keep your seat belts securely fastened." Dorothy watched as the stewardess sat down and put on her seat belt.

"Hurray!" shouted Harry. "Over and out!"

Mrs. Kane didn't bother to shush him, and every time the plane lurched and dipped, Harry issued another "Hurray!" Dorothy held on to her mother's hand and looked over at Chloe. She was holding on to Mr. Kane's hand, and her father's book was nowhere in sight.

The plane bounced once more, and when Harry yelled, "This is better than the roller coaster!" Mrs. Kane managed to utter one word to Harry. "Enough!" she said, between clenched teeth.

At last, the vibrating stopped, and the stewardess unhooked her seat belt and announced, "We will be landing shortly."

There was a strange noise, and Dorothy whispered to her mother, "What's that?"

Mrs. Kane said calmly, "Don't worry. That's only the landing gear, even if Harry is disappointed." She leaned over and kissed Harry on the cheek. "You enjoyed that, didn't you?" she said, laughing.

"It was the greatest!" said Harry. "Over and out!"

Dorothy could see trees that looked like little lollipops outside the window now, and there were lots of miniature houses with tiny swimming pools in their backyards. It wasn't until the airplane touched down on the runway and came to a complete stop that Dorothy realized she had swallowed her gum.

When Mr. Kane carried their luggage into Grandma's condominium, Dorothy thought it hardly looked like anyone lived there. Everything was shiny new. The couch had fifteen pillows so carefully arranged that Dorothy was afraid to sit down and lean against them. Harry changed all that. He piled the pillows as high as they could go and invited Dorothy to try to go higher. Grandma didn't say a word, so Dorothy piled while Chloe set the table for supper.

"It's only four o'clock!" said Chloe, looking at her watch.

"We like to eat early," said Grandpa, chuckling. "After supper, I'll give you a tour of the place."

While Grandma and Mrs. Kane stayed behind and drank coffee, Grandpa showed them around. Dorothy hadn't seen so many old people since her trip to the nursing home. They sat outside on benches. They sat around the swimming pool. They gathered in the recreation hall. Three old ladies were even showering in the pool bathroom.

"Some of them don't like to dirty their own bathrooms," said Grandpa, shaking his head when Dorothy told him. "So they use this one."

"A lizard!" cried Harry, when a tiny green

creature darted across the pathway. "Maybe I can catch one and bring it home!"

"It might be too fast for you, Harry," said Grandpa.

"And the stewardess wouldn't like it," said Dorothy.

When they reached the shuffleboard, Harry and Dorothy wanted to play, but Mr. Kane said they'd better get back to the apartment and unpack.

Grandma gave them each a kiss on the head and a drawer, and they emptied their suitcases. Afterward, Mr. Kane read his book while Grandma and Grandpa watched "Jeopardy" on television. Sometimes Mrs. Kane shouted out the answer from the kitchen, where she was reading the Florida newspaper.

Dorothy and Harry were just about to ask if they could go outside and play shuffleboard, when Mr. Kane slapped his book down on the table. "Is anyone hungry?" he said. "It's only six-thirty, and I need an ice-cream cone!"

115

"Hurray!" shouted Dorothy and Harry and Chloe. Grandma looked surprised and said she had some ice cream in the freezer, but Mr. Kane shook his head. So Grandma and Grandpa turned off the television, and the whole family went out to Rose's Luncheonette for ice-cream cones.

Chloe and Mr. Kane had their usual chocolate cones, and Mrs. Kane and Grandma chose peach. Harry stood in front of the big container of vanilla fudge.

"I'd like that part," said Harry, pointing to the ice cream with the biggest swirl of fudge in it.

Grandpa surprised everyone by choosing chocolate marshmallow with sprinkles, and Dorothy thought it looked so good that she joined him. They walked back to Grandma's condominium slowly, watching the palm trees swaying in the breeze, exclaiming over the beautiful flowers, licking their ice-cream cones fast enough so that the ice cream didn't drip down on their fingers.

"Isn't Florida great?" said Harry.

"It sure is," said Dorothy.

And then it started to rain.

It rained continuously for three days. Mr. Kane took them to the movies. They visited a museum. They walked around a shopping mall. They went to an indoor playground at the local McDonald's.

"We can do this at home," complained Harry, circling around and around on the carousel.

"I wish we could go swimming," said Dorothy behind Harry.

"I heard someone say it's snowing at home," said Chloe, looking over at Harry for his reaction.

Harry jumped off the carousel before it even stopped.

"Can we go home tomorrow?" said Harry to his mother. "I want to build a snowman. I need to. It's very important."

"We have two more days," said Mrs. Kane. "Maybe the sun will come out tomorrow."

117

"I won't go to any more shopping malls," said Harry grumpily.

"And no more museums," said Dorothy, joining him.

Chloe was kinder. "Maybe we can take a trip to Disney World," she suggested.

"I can't afford it," said Mr. Kane. "This year we're visiting Grandma and Grandpa. Maybe next year."

They spent the next morning reading books at the library. Mrs. Kane asked Chloe and Dorothy to read Harry a few stories. "I'm up to number seventeen," she explained, "and my voice is going."

"We can do this at home," complained Harry.

"I am *soooooo* bored," said Chloe, putting down a book on dinosaurs.

"Me, *tooooo,*" said Dorothy, copying Chloe's whine exactly, because actresses know how to do that.

"Enough," said Mr. and Mrs. Kane at the same time.

"I hate Florida," said Harry.

118

"So do I," said Dorothy.

Before Chloe could say anything, Mrs. Kane raised a finger. "Don't say it if you know what's good for you," she said.

Chloe kept her mouth shut.

"No swimming once," whispered Harry.

"And tomorrow is our last day," whispered Dorothy, but she stood up and returned a book to the shelf so that her mother couldn't catch her eye.

When Dorothy woke up the next day, she ran to the window. "The rain stopped!" she shouted to Harry. They opened up the front door and stuck out their hands.

"Cold," said Harry, disappointed.

"Oh," said Dorothy, making a face.

Dorothy's mother stepped outside and came back in. "Nasty!" she said, sounding as disappointed as Harry.

"I have an idea," said Dorothy, getting excited. "Let's pretend it's a beautiful sunny day. Let's go to the beach anyway!"

"But it looks like rain," said Harry.

"It's cold out there," said Chloe.

"I don't want you children getting sick," said Mrs. Kane doubtfully.

"It'll be great!" said Dorothy. "We can pack a picnic lunch, and dress warm, and sit on the sand!"

"I don't know, Dorothy," said her grandmother.

"Nobody listens to me, ever!" said Dorothy, banging so hard against the metal front door that it sounded like a drum. She opened the door halfway and turned. "Harry always gets what he wants, and Chloe always gets what she wants, and nobody listens to me at all!" Dorothy ran out the front door. "I'm playing shuffleboard," she yelled back. "Even if it starts to rain!"

Dorothy walked quickly in the direction of the shuffleboard court. The benches were empty, and the sidewalks were deserted. She passed the recreation hall, where a handful of old people were playing cards. Nobody was showering in the ladies' room.

Dorothy sat down on a bench. She didn't feel like asking the old man in the recreation hall for the shuffleboard equipment. He would probably say no. She was starting to shiver and wished she had brought along a sweater.

Her father brought one. He draped it around her shoulders and sat down next to her. "So you want to go to the beach?" he said.

Dorothy shrugged.

"I happen to think it's an excellent idea," said Mr. Kane.

"You do?" said Dorothy.

"I do," said Mr. Kane. "It seems to me that you're full of excellent ideas."

"I told you I was," said Dorothy, leaning her head against her father.

"So you did," said Mr. Kane, hugging her back.

"The sun might even come out today," said Dorothy hopefully.

"It might," said her father as they walked back to Grandma's condominium.

Grandma packed them tuna-fish sandwiches and fruit and cookies and a Thermos. Mr. Kane gathered up sweatshirts and towels and threw them into the back of the car.

"Should we put on our bathing suits?" said Dorothy.

"Of course," said Mrs. Kane. "We're going to the beach."

"Hurray!" said Harry, pulling open his drawer and rummaging in it for his dinosaur trunks. "Grandma, would you like to go swimming with me?"

Grandma laughed and linked arms with Grandpa. "We'll stay home and make you a great fish dinner," she said.

The beach was deserted. Mr. Kane turned to Dorothy and said, "Where would you like me to spread the blanket?"

Dorothy chose a spot, and everybody took off their shoes and quickly placed them on the edges of the blanket to keep it from blowing away. Harry was the first one to reach the water.

"It's freezing!" he shouted as he raced away from the waves. Dorothy and Chloe ran with him, screaming when they weren't fast enough and the water hit their toes.

Mr. Kane pulled out buckets and shovels and said, "Who would like to build the most fantastic castle you've ever seen in your life?"

"Me!" shouted Dorothy and Harry and Chloe, and they grabbed their shovels and started digging. The sand was heavy and wet and just right for building castles.

Mrs. Kane took out her camera and posed the family around the castle when it was almost finished. She looked through the window of the camera and started to laugh. "You all look so funny!" she said between giggles. Dorothy looked at Harry. Beneath his sweatshirt hood, all she could see was the tip of his nose and his tongue sticking out from the corner of his mouth as he smoothed the castle walls. Chloe had on her shiny new sunglasses, but there was no sun. Mr. Kane had a bandanna tied around his head and a shovel in each hand as he put the finishing touches on the moat.

Dorothy sprang up and started to sing, "Rain, rain, go away, we're in Florida for our last day!" She danced around the sand castle until her father jumped up and joined her, dancing wildly with a shovel in each hand. Then Harry and Chloe and Mrs. Kane followed, laughing and singing and dancing, while the gulls circled overhead, screeching at them from the dark Florida sky.

The singing and dancing and digging made them hungry. Mrs. Kane unpacked the sandwiches and fruit and cookies and said, "Let's eat!"

"This is the best lunch ever," said Dorothy, munching hungrily on her tuna-fish sandwich. Harry discovered that the Thermos had hot chocolate in it instead of coffee. He shouted, "Hurray!" so loudly that his mother screamed, and the whole family started laughing again.

The plane ride home was at night, and each of the children was given a pillow. Dorothy felt very grown-up, because already this was her second ride on an airplane. As the engine started roaring, Dorothy kept her hands on the armrests. She didn't even need to hold her mother's hand. At last the airplane was flying smoothly through the sky. Dorothy fished in her pocketbook for her new packet of gum. That's when she found her unfinished letter to Jessica. She took out her purple felt-tip pen, turned the letter over, and wrote: *P.S. Now we are going home. Florida was rainy and cold. We went to the beach anyway. It was grate. My dad says we got coldburn instead of sunburn. Love, Dorothy.*

Dorothy put the letter back into the envelope and sealed it. When she got home, she would mail it to Jessica. Jessica would like getting a letter.

Chloe was napping, and Dorothy settled her pillow against her mother and closed her eyes. Harry kept himself awake.

"I want to see if there's any snow," he told Mrs. Kane.

As the airplane wheels touched down on the

runway, Harry shouted his final "Hurray!" and woke his sisters up. They gathered up their belongings and followed the crowd off the plane.

Dorothy and Harry found their father an empty cart, and he went to get the luggage. They put on their winter jackets. When the automatic doors slid open, the cold night air hit them.

They stepped outside. "Home, sweet home," said Mrs. Kane.

"Work tomorrow," said Mr. Kane.

"It's snowing!" said Harry.

Dorothy had an idea. She was full of excellent ideas. "Tomorrow," she said, taking hold of Harry's hand, "we'll build the best snowman in the world."

And they did.

7

The Snowball War

DOROTHY AND HARRY built the tallest snowman on the block, even taller than the one Benny Spignolli and his older and bigger brother built a few doors away. According to Dorothy's father, not only was it the tallest, but it was the most original.

"That snowman has enormous character,"

said Mr. Kane, standing on the front porch. "He reminds me of someone."

Mrs. Kane joined him. "Me, too," she said. "I love the old fedora hat and the heavy eyebrows."

"We used pieces of black crayon for those," said Dorothy proudly. "And Grandpa's hat."

"That's who it reminds me of!" said Mr. Kane. "Grandpa Leon!"

"That's who it is!" cried Dorothy, because it sounded like such a good idea, and because it did look a lot like Grandpa.

"Benny Spignolli made a good snowman," said Chloe, crowding onto the front porch for a look. "It looks just like him."

"It's a fat snowman," said Harry matter-of-factly. "And it's kind of mean-looking."

"I guess it's fat like Benny," said Chloe.

"And mean like Benny," said Dorothy.

"That's not nice," said Mrs. Kane, shivering on the doorstep. "I'm going back inside."

"It's the truth," said Chloe, following her mother.

Harry turned to Dorothy. "Well, our snowman has a great personality," he said.

"Like Grandpa," said Dorothy. She tilted the fedora slightly and stepped back. "Grandpa wears it like that," she added.

"And Grandpa loves hot chocolate," said Harry, heading inside.

"I take after Grandpa," shouted Dorothy as she rushed after him. "We both like marshmallows floating in our cup!"

After school the following day, Dorothy and Harry lagged behind their mother.

"Are you two staying outside?" called Mrs. Kane. "You can play in the front yard."

"Okay!" called Dorothy. "We're just going to check out Benny Spignolli's snowman again."

It *was* a fat snowman. He had a stocking cap on his head, bottle-cap eyes, and a carrot stick laid sideways for his mouth.

"Coca-Cola eyes," said Harry observantly. "And he's definitely mean-looking."

"But he has Pepsi bottle-cap buttons," said Dorothy.

"Our snowman has much more personality," said Harry.

"Who says so?" called a voice from behind a large fir tree.

"I do," said Harry. "Our snowman looks like Grandpa Leon."

"Your Grandpa Leon is a jerk, then," said Benny Spignolli, stepping out from behind the tree.

"Take that back," said Harry.

"Who's going to make me?" said Benny, doubling up his fists and squinting his eyes so that his cheeks puffed out, which Dorothy couldn't help noticing were very fat.

"Let's go," said Dorothy, pulling at Harry's jacket.

"Chicken," called Benny as they walked away.

"We are not!" said Dorothy, hoping that she had a fierce expression on her face as she turned to face Benny.

That's when the snowball war began. A big fat round snowball hit Dorothy's cheek with such force that she slipped on the sidewalk and fell right on her backside.

"Creep!" called Dorothy, tears springing to her eyes. She swiped them away with her mittens, but not before Harry saw.

Harry headed back toward Benny, but he was so bombarded by snowballs that he had to shield his face.

Dorothy hastily dusted off her bottom and went to help Harry. Her heart was beating worse than when she had stage fright, because she didn't really know what she would do when she reached Benny Spignolli, and besides, being hit by a snowball hurt. A fat one hit her on the shoulder, and it was only then that she noticed Benny's brother Carl. Carl was twice as big as Benny, and so were his snowballs.

"Come on, Harry," said Dorothy desperately. "His brother is there."

"I'll fight them with my eyes closed," said Harry. "I'll fight them with one hand tied behind my back."

Dorothy didn't really think it was the best time for Harry to pretend he was the Cowardly Lion from *The Wizard of Oz,* but when she heard

Carl Spignolli call out, "My ice ball is awesome. It feels just like a baseball," she ran like he was the Wicked Witch. And Harry the Cowardly Lion Kane followed.

They didn't tell Mrs. Kane about the snowball war. Mostly because they hoped it would be over by the morning.

But it wasn't. And to make matters worse, it had snowed some more during the night.

Harry and Dorothy stuck close to their mother as she walked them to school. When the first snowball whacked Harry in the back, only Dorothy noticed. But when the second snowball hit Dorothy on the shoulder, Chloe said, "Who's throwing those snowballs?" very loudly.

Mrs. Kane turned around, and Benny and Carl disappeared behind a parked car. "Juvenile delinquents," she said, and she herded the children together.

On the way home from school, Dorothy was jumpy. Harry made believe he was an airplane. Dorothy thought maybe he wasn't as afraid of ice snowballs as she was. The swishing of car tires in the street, the click of a front door opening, a dog barking ... every noise made her jump. Harry wasn't a bit worried. He even wanted to play outside.

"Not me," said Dorothy. She could find the way out of the woods for her family. She could tell great stories in front of her class. She could even ride on an airplane without holding her mother's hand. But she couldn't, she just couldn't, pretend she wasn't afraid of snowballs. She was chicken, just like Benny had said. Dorothy went inside.

Harry came in a few minutes later, with a very red chin. "They got me in the face," he whispered to Dorothy. "Don't tell Mom."

Harry and Dorothy played in Dorothy's bedroom. Dorothy made Harry a snack in her play kitchen. She gave him a dish of fake ice cream, big round plastic scoops that Grandma had given her for her birthday that looked and smelled just like real ice cream.

Harry made believe he was eating with a loud

slurping sound. Then he stopped. He pushed away the dish of ice cream.

"I don't want any more," he said. "It reminds me of snowballs."

Dorothy had to agree. She cleared off the table and told Harry she was his teacher. "It's time for arts and crafts," she said, taking out a basket of paper and glue and crayons and a bag of pompons. She gave Harry a piece of paper.

"I'd like some pompons," said Harry, cheering up a little.

Dorothy handed him six pompons, because Harry tended to waste them. He never stuck them on with enough glue, and then they ended up rolling under the bed.

Harry and Dorothy drew and pasted. Dorothy made a flower garden and chose a different color pompon for each flower. Then she drew petals around each one. Harry made a picture of two little people with the six pompons circling their heads. He glued them on carefully and didn't waste a single one.

"Very nice," said Dorothy the teacher. "What is it?"

"It's you and me being hit by snowballs," said Harry.

"Who's throwing them?" said Dorothy.

Harry set to work. He was concentrating so hard that his tongue stuck out of the corner of his mouth. "There," he said, drawing two huge snow-men on the left-hand side of the picture. "Two abominable snowmen are bothering them."

"Are they supposed to be Benny and Carl?" asked Dorothy.

Harry shrugged his shoulders.

During supper, Dorothy and Harry were very quiet. Mr. Kane noticed. "Hey, you two," he said. "Why so silent?"

Dorothy turned her mouth up at the edges, but she knew you couldn't really call it a smile. Harry played with his boiled potato, which he had already whispered to Dorothy reminded him of a snowball. Dorothy agreed, but she mashed hers up and put some butter on it, and it didn't

135

taste anything like a snowball. She knew what Harry meant, anyway.

Chloe blabbed. "Benny Spignolli and his big brother are bothering them."

"Say that three times fast," said Mr. Kane, laughing, but nobody laughed back.

"Are they still throwing snowballs?" said Mrs. Kane. "I'm going to talk to their mother."

"Don't do that," said Dorothy quickly. Sometimes when she passed the Spignolli house, she heard Benny's mother yelling at him. Maybe if Mrs. Kane talked to Benny's mother he would stop throwing snowballs. But maybe in the springtime he would throw rocks! And maybe in the summertime he would catch the biggest bumblebees and yellow jackets he could find, and he'd open up the jar when she passed his house! And maybe in the autumn he would jump out at her in the scariest Halloween costume he could find! "Don't say a word to his mother," Dorothy said firmly.

"We'll see," said Mrs. Kane.

Harry piped up. "I've decided," he said. "I'm going to make my own ice balls. If I bring in my own snowballs and put them in the freezer, they'll be harder than Benny's brother's awesome ice balls."

"They feel like baseballs," added Dorothy.

"Oh, great," said Mrs. Kane. "Harry, throwing ice balls will make you just as bad as they are."

"But I'll feel better," said Harry.

Dorothy saw her father wipe away a smile by dabbing at his mouth with a napkin. "We'll figure something out," he said to Mrs. Kane. "The peaceful way."

"Like Mahatma Gandhi," said Chloe. "We learned about Gandhi in school the other day."

"He let people hit him with snowballs?" said Harry.

"I don't think so," said Chloe. "But he didn't fight back."

"He didn't believe in violence to make change," said Mr. Kane. "It's called passive resistance. He turned the other cheek."

"Snowballs hurt," said Dorothy, remembering the very snowball that hit her on the cheek, but it felt good to be talking about it.

"We'll think of something," said her father once more.

Harry must have felt better, too, because when his mother offered him a bowl of vanilla fudge ice cream, he didn't complain that the scoops looked too much like snowballs. And if his mother hadn't stopped him, he would have licked the bowl.

That night, Dorothy had a terrible dream. She was walking through a dark forest, and there was a boy that looked like Benny Spignolli behind every tree. A snowball hit her in the head, and when she bent to pick it up, a snowball hit her in the backside. She turned to look at the boy behind the nearest tree, and he had a baseball bat in his hand and a bucket of ice cubes.

"That's why they're called ice balls," said Dorothy as she watched Benny insert an ice cube into every snowball. She walked as fast as she could and came to another ice bucket. "I'll make my own ice balls," said Dorothy, but when she took the cover off, the bucket was empty.

"Ice, ice, I need some ice!" shouted Dorothy, and she woke up.

Her mother came running into the room. "What's the matter, honey, do you have a fever? I heard you say you need ice."

"No," said Dorothy, glad that she was in her own bed in her own room. "I'll just have a drink of water."

It was snowing heavily the next morning, and Dorothy and Harry and Chloe gathered around the radio listening to school closings.

Mrs. Kane looked up at the kitchen clock. "It looks like Walnut School is open," she said firmly. "Let's go."

They put on their jackets and scarves and hats and boots and started down the street. The roads and trees and sidewalks were covered in white, because nobody was out shoveling yet.

"It's so pretty," whispered Dorothy, forgetting all about Benny's snowball war—until a snowball whizzed through the air and hit the ground in front of her.

Dorothy's mother turned around so quickly that Benny Spignolli had no time to hide. She ran as fast as she could through the thick snow, and Benny turned around and ran away from her faster. "I'm going to tell your mother about this!" shouted Dorothy's mother.

Dorothy worried about it all day in school. When Mrs. Greenaway told her that the snowflake she had made was beautiful, she barely smiled. She thought she could hear Benny Spignolli a few seats behind her making funny noises. She wished that she lived far away like some of the other children. Their mothers had kept them out of school, because it was still snowing. Dorothy wished her seat was empty, too, like her best friend Jessica's, except that she wished that she was home making cookies with her mother, instead of home with a cold like Jessica.

Lunchtime, Dorothy sat with Andrea, who talked a lot more than Jessica.

"See my nail polish with the sparkles in it?" said Andrea, holding out a hand. "My stepmother, Gina, bought it for me, but she says I don't have to call her Mom, because I have a mom."

"It's pretty," said Dorothy, searching in her lunch box for dessert. "Raisins," she said out loud. "Yick."

"Have a chocolate chunk cookie," said Andrea, holding out a bag. "I made them with Gina. Gina gave me lipstick, too, but my mother said I couldn't wear it to school."

"My mother doesn't let me wear it to school, either," said Dorothy, munching on the cookie and feeling a lot better until Andrea said that it was still snowing outside.

"I hate snow," said Dorothy, with such feeling that Andrea looked surprised.

"Really?" she said. "I love it. Gina took me ice skating the other day."

Dorothy was about to tell her that she didn't feel like hearing about Gina anymore, when she felt something hit her on the shoulder. She looked down at the floor, half expecting to see a snowball.

Andrea looked, too. "It's an apple core," she said. "Whoever threw that is a real pig."

"Shhhh," said Dorothy, glancing over her shoulder to see if Benny Spignolli was anywhere in sight.

"Is somebody picking on you?" said Andrea. "Gina told me that sometimes if somebody is picking on you, it means they like you. Should we go tell Mrs. Greenaway?"

Dorothy shook her head. "It's only an old apple core," she said, looking out the window at the falling snow. If she wasn't feeling so miserable, she would have laughed at the idea of Benny liking her.

When the bell rang, Dorothy went to the school entrance to wait for her mother. Harry was already there, making disgusting burping noises with his best friend Benjamin. Chloe was talking to her friends and pretending that Harry was really some creature from outer space and not her brother.

"Mom's late," she said as Dorothy joined her.

"Some babies have to walk home with their mommies," said a loud voice. Dorothy knew the voice well. She stiffened up her shoulders. Harry stopped burping.

Someone was coming up the steps, someone very familiar to Dorothy, dressed in his letter carrier's uniform and carrying his blue pouch.

"It's Dad!" said Dorothy as her father pushed open the door, a gust of wind and snow hitting her.

"That's my dad," said Harry, and he threw down his knapsack and wrapped his arms around his father.

Dorothy heard some of the children whisper, "Their father's a mailman!" and she heard Joshua from her class say, "That's so neat!"

"Special delivery!" said Mr. Kane, and he pulled a bag of marshmallows out of his mail pouch and handed it to Dorothy. "Why don't you give them out to your friends?" he said.

Dorothy held the bag out to Andrea, and An-

drea took one. "Take another one," said Dorothy. "For Gina."

"Thanks," said Andrea, "but I'll take one for
my mother."

Dorothy held the bag out to Joshua, but Joshua
shook his head and said he wasn't hungry.

"Take one and keep it for your hot chocolate,"
Dorothy suggested.

"Great idea," said Joshua, and he put one in
his pocket.

Harry grabbed some for himself and for Benjamin, and Dorothy went to join her father. She
thought he looked very tall and handsome in his
uniform.

"Let's go brave the elements," said Mr. Kane,
giving Dorothy a big smile.

Dorothy took his hand proudly and turned to
see who was watching. Benny Spignolli was right
behind them, and her heart began to hammer.

That's when she remembered Mahatma Gandhi.
And she remembered what Andrea's stepmother,
Gina, had said. And that's when she had the

idea. She held out the marshmallow bag to Benny and said in the friendliest voice she could muster, "Would you like one?"

Benny looked surprised. He eyed the bag suspiciously. Then he reached inside the bag and took one.

"Take one for Carl, too," said Dorothy. Her heart was beginning to slow down.

"Carl isn't home," said Benny, swallowing his marshmallow.

"Then take one for your hot chocolate," said Dorothy.

"We don't have any hot chocolate in the house," said Benny, but he grabbed one anyway. Then he pushed the door open and headed down the stairs.

Dorothy and Harry and Chloe and her father followed him. The frigid air hit them as they walked down the steps, and Dorothy's father stopped to wrap her scarf more snugly around her.

"That was sweet of you, honey," he whispered.

Dorothy smiled. Then she had her best idea of all. "Benny!" she called loudly.

Benny stopped and turned. "What?" he said.

"Why don't you come back to our house for hot chocolate?" called Dorothy.

And Harry added, "My father makes it great! Come on!"

Benny hesitated. Then he mumbled, "I don't think so," and he turned and headed in the direction of his house.

When they reached the Spignolli home, Mr. Kane called out, "I see you built a fine snowman there, Benny. He's so big, he looks like a prize-fighter."

"That's not what he's supposed to be," said Benny, anchoring the bottle-cap nose more firmly in the snowman's face. "It's my father," added Benny. His voice got so low that Dorothy could barely hear him. "But he taught me boxing, before he got sick."

"I'll bet a big fellow like you can pack a mean wallop," said Mr. Kane.

146

"My dad told me I had a great right hook," said Benny.

Harry piped up. "Could you show me?" he said.

"My father used to be a boxer," said Dorothy. "At school. Didn't you, Dad?"

"A wrestler," said Mr. Kane. "But I've got a great book on boxing I could show you."

"Come on, Benny," said Dorothy, standing next to him now.

Benny hesitated. Finally he said, "Does it have any pictures of Muhammed Ali?"

Mr. Kane laughed. "Right on the jacket," he said. "Why don't you leave a note for your mother?"

Benny disappeared inside. Dorothy looked at the fat snowman. It didn't look as fat anymore. And it didn't look as mean.

She turned to her father. His cheeks were pink with the cold. "Do you think he died?" she said. "Benny's father?"

"I don't know, honey," said her father gently.

147

Benny joined them again, and they trudged down the street to the Kane house.

"Boots on the mat!" called Mrs. Kane when she heard the door open. She stopped dead in her tracks when she saw Benny, but she added, "Hello, Benny."

The kitchen was warm and cozy as they gathered around the table. A bowl of popcorn was already there, and a can of cocoa sat waiting.

Mr. Kane pried open the container and spooned some brown powder into a saucepan of steaming milk. He took a wooden spoon out of the drawer and stirred. Then he put on a fish-shaped pot holder and poured some of the hot milk into each cup. "Drink up," he said.

"Wait!" said Benny, so loudly that he made Dorothy jump. Benny fished in his pocket and pulled out his marshmallow. Then he dropped it in his cup.

"I like it that way, too," said Dorothy as her father took the bag of remaining marshmallows from his mailbag. Mr. Kane dropped two of them into Dorothy's cup, two more into Harry's, skipped Chloe altogether because he knew she didn't eat them, and put another one in Benny's. The children watched the bobbing marshmallows and waited while they melted into a white cream. Then they blew on their cups and drank.

"Mmm," said Benny, downing his drink in long gulps.

"The best," said Dorothy, taking smaller sips. "Would you like to play a game or something now?"

Harry drained his cup almost as fast as Benny did and left the room. When he came back, he was carrying a board game.

"Let's play," he said, pushing aside the popcorn bowl and setting up the game.

They played for a while, until Mrs. Kane said to Benny, "Would you like to stay for dinner? I can give your mother a call."

"My mom's at work," said Benny. "Carl makes me something."

"It's chicken," said Dorothy, sniffing at the

aroma coming from the oven. She looked at Benny's face. It still looked fat to her, but not fat and disgusting. It looked more like a Cabbage Patch doll. "You can have the leg," Dorothy added. "That's my favorite."

"Okay," said Benny, and he gave her a smile that puffed out his cheeks, but this time there was a dimple in each one of them that Dorothy had never seen before.

"Harry, you can clear the table, and Benny, you can help Dorothy set," said Mrs. Kane, handing him a stack of plates. "Are they too heavy for you?"

"He's very strong," said Dorothy, remembering that he threw a mean wallop of a snowball, too.

"He's a boxer," said Harry.

"Really?" said Mrs. Kane.

"His father taught him," said Harry. "And after supper he's going to teach me."

"Me, too," said Dorothy, and she looked at Benny. He screwed up his eyes and blinked them, and for a moment Dorothy wondered if he was going to cry.

Benny smiled again instead, an ear-to-ear smile that was bigger than the last one. "You never know when you might need to belt someone," he said. "If they get out of line or something." His voice trailed off, and Dorothy wondered if he was talking about himself. Maybe she could pretend she was the best female prizefighter after dinner.

"We don't believe in hitting," said Mrs. Kane softly.

"Have you ever heard of Mahatma Gandhi?" said Harry.

"Nope," said Benny. "Was he a boxer?"

"He didn't believe in violence," said Chloe.

"Oh," said Benny, looking down at the kitchen table. "Sorry about that."

Benny had three pieces of chicken and one and a half baked potatoes with lots of butter. Dorothy was surprised to see him eat all of his string beans and ask for some more.

After supper, Mr. Kane handed Benny a book and said, "You can keep this." Then he put on his boots and jacket and said, "I'll walk you home, Benny. It's dark outside."

"Can I come, too?" said Dorothy.

"Dress warmly," said her father.

"What about my boxing lesson?" said Harry.

"Another day," said Mr. Kane, waiting for Benny and Dorothy to put on their jackets.

The snow was sparkling white in the light of the street lamps as they stepped outside. Dorothy thought it had never looked so pretty. They walked without talking and reached Benny's house. Benny stood at the front door, stamping his feet on the snow-covered porch.

"Well," he said, "I guess I'll see you at school tomorrow." He waved the book at them. "Thanks for the book and the food and everything."

"You're welcome," said Mr. Kane.

"Good-bye," said Dorothy, taking her father's hand as they walked back down the snowy sidewalk.

Benny called after them, "You've got a neat family!"

"Thanks!" said Dorothy, waving at him. Suddenly she heard a shout, coming from the direction of her house. It was Harry.

"What's the matter?" called Benny from half-way inside the house.

Dorothy laughed. "Harry wants to know if you can show him how to make an ice ball," she said.

"Tell him, tomorrow," said Benny. Dorothy could hear him laughing as he closed the door.

Mr. Kane and Dorothy turned up the walkway to their house. Through the picture window, Dorothy could see Robin Redbreast, nesting happily in his potted tree. Her mother passed through the living room, and Harry followed. It looked as if he was practicing his right hook, or maybe he was throwing snowballs.

Dorothy squeezed her father's hand, and he squeezed back.

"We do have a nice family, don't we?" said Dorothy.

"The best," said Mr. Kane, opening up the front door.

Dorothy took off her wet boots and left on her socks. She walked into the kitchen. Clean pots and dishes were dripping on the dish drainer. She would surprise her mother and dry them without even being asked. Then she would call Jessica to see if she was feeling any better. Maybe Jessica could come over after school the next day, and they could write a play about two princesses who find out that a fat dragon is really a prince. Or something like that.

Dorothy picked up the dish towel and carefully lifted the stainless steel pot off the pile of dishes it was resting on. She polished it over and over until she could see her reflection in it. It was a nice face, she thought. A smart face, too. The face of a person with excellent ideas.

Dorothy could hear Harry and Chloe in the living room, singing a song from *The Wizard of Oz*. It was nice having a brother and sister, even if she *was* the one in the middle. After all, if she wanted to be the only kid in the house, she could always pretend.

"We need you, Dorothy!" Harry called from the living room. "It's your turn to sing!" And Dorothy ran to join them, sliding across the living room floor in her socks.

9·92